A Distant Dream

Lynette Rees

LYNETTE REES

Prologue

Two surprising things happened following Cassandra's marriage to Harry Hewitt. The first being that Harry was called in to attend the inquest for the Marshfield Pit Explosion and the other, that he'd been contacted afterwards by the pit owner Josiah Wilkinson's eldest son, James.

Josiah arrived at the colliery at one p.m. two weeks before the disaster and went down the pit with the manager, foreman and other officials. A strange odour was detected by some of the colliers which Mr Wilkinson dismissed as he had said, 'No canary has dropped off its perch!' which was found to be true at the time but did not ease the men's minds.

Two more inspections were made the following week when Mr Wilkinson was accompanied by officials and several colliers were present.

In his report the Inspector commented:

From the evidence, *No men should have been allowed to work the lower side of the middle level until the gas had been cleared away which should have been detected not dismissed. In my opinion, there was a build-up of gas which was ignited and was the cause of the sad explosion, but as locked safety lamps are employed at the pit, I am unable to ascertain whether a naked light, defective lamp or improper use of one, fired the gas, hence causing the explosion. The pit owner, Josiah Samuel Wilkinson, had been alerted by the men via the foreman, Tom Langstone and manager, William Hewitt, two weeks previously of their suspicions of underground gas which alas was ignored by the owner of the pit.*

As a result of the evidence given, a verdict of manslaughter against the pit owner, Josiah Samuel Wilkinson, was awarded. After hearing all the evidence the judge said there was no case against either the foreman or the manager who were both found not guilty of negligence.

As two members of the party mentioned were already deceased, the third, Tom Langstone, at being cleared of manslaughter, did not jump for joy. He'd already been left a life sentence to contend with even though folk were treating him as a hero as he'd returned to the pit to try to find the young lad. He'd lost the best manager the pit had ever had and that particular day, he'd also lost his peace of mind.

Chapter One

May 1876

Cassandra sat in the living room of the cottage and gazed around her. It was looking nice and cosy here now after Polly and Rose Barton had helped her to clean it all up after Jem and Clyde had moved their furniture and all their knick-knacks over to Hewitt Hall. It was only a temporary measure for her living at the cottage as Harry planned on buying them a suitable home of their own as soon as possible. Emily was at school and so, today, Cassie had the chance to put her feet up for a while, but she was restless. Something inside her made it hard for her to sit still. She'd spent the morning sweeping the carpets, polishing the furniture and buffing the brass until everything shone. The beds were stripped, windows opened and bedding washed. Now, she was ready to peg the washing out on the line, and as it was a sunny, breezy day, she intended to make the most of it. It was the sort of day when the washing would flap around happily in the breeze. It was hard work washing all their clothing and the dirty bed linen in the dolly tub too, but she'd persevered as she wanted the place like a sparkling new pin when Harry arrived home after the inquest.

His father's death had taken a toll on him of late she realised, at the back of his mind was the feeling of betrayal towards him and his mother. He was more than happy for Clyde to inherit Hewitt Hall as he felt the young man had endured a difficult start in life and missed out on what he had experienced growing up: a comfortable home and even the chance to study at Oxford University. Even though he'd made a hash of that. It was more the fact that he hadn't seen this coming by a long chalk. It was almost as if his father was hurting both him and his mother from beyond the grave.

Edna, though, seemed more than happy living with Polly and Aunt Bertha at Hawthorn Cottage until her cottage at Drisdale was fully repaired and decorated ready for her to move into. It seemed unfair that she'd had to move into such a small place while his father's mistress got a bigger property. He supposed it just illuminated the fact of how little his father had cared for his mother in the end.

Cassie hefted the wicker basket of washed laundry out to the clothesline, huffing and puffing as she did so. She set the basket down on a paving stone near the rope line and bent down to lift one of Harry's shirts when she felt a sudden twinge. Immediately, her hands flew to her abdomen and she gasped at the sharpness of the pain. Leaving the discarded basket, she made her way slowly back to the cottage, dragging her feet as she went. The twins weren't due for another couple of weeks Doctor Bryant thought and so did she. She settled herself down by the fire and breathed in and out deeply until the pain had passed over. There was no doubt about it, she was going into labour. Harry was due back at any time, so she hoped he'd return soon and fetch the doctor to her.

***

Harry and James were seated opposite one another at The Swan Hotel in Hocklea, they were in the bar area which was open to the general public. Today, it was fairly busy but they'd managed to acquire a table near the window in a little alcove where they could speak in private with one another.

Harry, although still extremely upset by everything, had decided he'd attend to hear what the man had to say to him following the inquest. After all, James had lost his father too in a horrific manner so they had much in common. Josiah Wilkinson had travelled to France and sitting in his hotel room, had pulled out his pistol and blown his brains out for his negligence at the pit that caused the disaster in the first place. No matter what Harry thought of Josiah, he had no quarrel with his son.

James summoned a barman over to their table who took their orders of a glass of brandy each. 'I think we both need these,' said James forcing a smile.

Harry nodded but did not say anything. The truth was he didn't know what to say. He watched James who appeared to be as nervous as he was as he ran a finger under the stiff collar of his white pristine shirt as if it were too tight for him.

Finally, James said meeting his gaze, 'You're probably wondering why I brought you here today?'

Harry nodded. 'Yes.'

'It's not to waste your time. It's to put a proposition forward.' James drained his glass and ordered two more for them.

'A proposition?' Harry sat forward in his seat, noticing the guarded look in James's eyes.

'Yes. We are both suffering over the pit explosion, though in different ways...' He licked his lips. 'Anyhow, it's been put to me by my father's legal team that I'm due to inherit Marshfield Coal Pit.' He shrugged his shoulders. 'I don't have the first clue about that sort of thing nor much interest, to be honest with you, but one thing I would like to do is improve conditions there for the men and boys so that an accident like that shouldn't occur again. I'd like to improve safety measures, give them all a raise, within reason, look into who is working there overseeing running the pit and if they ought to be replaced, etcetera.'

'But I don't see what all of this has to do with me?' Harry felt bewildered and frowned.

James caught his eye. 'I'd like to have you on

board with me. I want some good to come out of this.'

'But I still don't see how I can possibly help you? I don't know the first thing about the workings of a coal pit.'

'You wouldn't have to. At least not to begin with. We can bring in experts and other professionals to help us. I'm offering you a half share in the pit. Half of my inheritance!'

Harry shook his head. 'I don't know what to say, to be honest. It's not what I was expecting. I've never had any interest in any pits or mines, though I have been left some shares in a lead mine in Hackingdale that was passed on to me after my father's death. But that is most generous of you.'

'Look, just say you'll think about it. It would be my way to make amends for my father's negligence.'

'It seems,' said Harry, 'that we both had fathers who let us down.'

James raised a puzzled brow. 'What did your father do then? I thought he was revered by the men at the pit?'

'Oh, he was...' Harry smiled sardonically. 'I won't go into it all but let's just say after his death, mother and I felt a little betrayed. Maybe I'll tell you someday.'

James nodded knowingly as if being let down by one's father happened every day. 'I won't pry, but I've heard no gossip since your father's death.'

'No, but it will all come out soon enough,' Harry

said realising that Clyde's parentage could not be kept a secret for much longer. 'Let's just say I have a half-brother I knew nothing about.' He stared out of the window at the passing trade outside in the street. All the world just carried on as if two of the once most respected men in the area had not passed away at all. Life stopped for no man, he realised. Jolting himself out of his reverie, he looked at James. 'Isn't there a second pit too?'

'Yes. My brother has inherited that one. It's about twenty miles away in Blackheath, a much smaller concern than Marshfield Pit.'

The brandy was beginning to warm Harry's blood and he smiled at James. The man had done him no harm whatsoever and appeared to want to do him some good which he was grateful for. 'Let's order something to eat,' he said decisively and James nodded. It wouldn't harm either of them to have a chat about the future of Marshfield Pit.

***

The contractions were now coming fast and furiously for Cassie. Oh, no, was she about to give birth all alone on the floor in front of the fireside? Would she now be in danger as it was a twin birth? So many questions were running through her mind, she tried to calm herself down by breathing and exhaling deeply. Suddenly, she heard a voice. 'Coo-ee!' Polly! She was never so glad to hear the woman's voice in all her born days.

'O...over here, Pol!' Cassie gasped. 'I think the babies are coming and Harry hasn't arrived h...

home yet!'

'Oh, my word!' Polly appeared in the doorway, her eyes enlarged with horror. 'Now, you try to relax. I'll put the kettle on to boil. Then I'll be right back.'

She bent down to lift the kettle from near the fireside and went off to fill it with water from the pump in the back yard then she settled it onto the flames of the fire. Kneeling beside Cassie she soothed, 'Now, let's get you comfortable. I'll fetch a few pillows from upstairs and some blankets. Where do you keep your towels?'

'There's a cupboard upstairs where you'll find them, just on the landing.'

Polly returned sometime later with a pile of blankets, pillows and towels and she set them down on the scrubbed pine table. 'Are you feeling the need to push?' She asked with concern in her voice.

Cassie nodded and closing her eyes bit her lower lip. The pains were coming again, rippling across her abdomen and she cried out like a wounded animal.

Polly took her hand. 'Here, squeeze my hand if you need to,' she said kindly. 'But first I'm going to wet a flannel with cool water to soothe your brow. I'm sure Harry won't be much longer, then we can get the doctor out to you.'

It was all very well Polly trying to reassure her that Harry would be back soon but where the hell was he? He should have been back by now. Cassie opened her mouth to let out a loud, guttural scream which seemed to be coming from elsewhere, rather like a wounded animal crying out in pain.

Chapter Two

Harry had lost track of how many brandies he'd consumed. Thankfully, James had offered him a lift home later. There was no real rush to return and they were getting along famously. It was almost as though through their shared commonality of losing their fathers in such a tragic fashion that they'd bonded, maybe they wouldn't become as close as Harry had become to Clyde or Jem of late but nevertheless, they seemed to have a mutual understanding and wanted to improve the conditions for the workers at the Marshfield Coal Pit to avoid any further disasters in the future.

'Here, have a cigar, old chap!' James was saying to him as he passed one across the table. Harry hesitated before accepting one, he didn't usually smoke but it was a special occasion after all. Perhaps he would have another drink, it wasn't every day that he went into business with someone else. Although he hated the man's father for killing his own and also taking the life of young Benny Brewster in that pit explosion, he felt no malice whatsoever towards his son—after all, he was just as much a victim of his father's selfishness as Harry was of his own father's.

A waiter appeared by the table and extracted a box of matches from his pocket and lit their cigars for them. Harry nodded his appreciation at the man and closing his eyes, drew on the cigar, just savouring the moment. His eyes flicked open as he blew out a grey plume of smoke as he noticed James appeared to be gazing at him with avid interest. 'Any problem?' he asked furrowing his brow.

'No, none at all. I was just thinking what a lucky man you are to have married the lovely Cassandra Bellingham. I knew her when she was previously married to the Lord. My father was great friends with him.'

'I see,' said Harry frowning fully now. What was the man getting at? Was he trying to be funny with him?

James let out a little chuckle. 'Relax, my fine fellow. I was not about to besmirch your good wife, she's had plenty of trouble from folk, I realise that. I meant what I said, she's a pearl amongst pebbles in this area...'

'Or amongst swine!' said Harry, surprising himself with his outburst of vehemence.

'Hang on there,' James soothed. 'I know the villagers in these parts behaved badly towards her but now they seem to have accepted her as one of their own.'

Harry softened. It was true, even his mother who had viewed Cassandra as her arch-enemy had finally dissolved and fallen in love with her. These days they were as close as mother and daughter and it gladdened his heart. 'You are correct of course, I just feel so protective of her especially now that she's ...'

James quirked a brow. 'Now she's expecting? I had heard.'

'Yes. Of course, the babies are not mine, they are his lordship's offspring,' he said nonchalantly.

'And does that bother you at all? That the babies will not be your own flesh and blood?'

'No,' he shook his head. 'Not at all because the twins will be part of Cassandra, the woman I love. I already love her daughter, Emily, too. So it's not that I can't or won't accept another man's child or children.'

'Then what is it?' James cocked his head to one side.

Harry let out a long, audible sigh. 'I suppose I'd like us to have our own child someday, but I fear that will not be possible. Three children will be enough for any woman.'

James grinned. 'Don't you believe it. Many women love to have a houseful of sprogs around the place, hanging off their pinafores.'

Harry returned the smile but he very much doubted that. 'The thing is Cassandra still wants to run her own tea room, she's very independent you know—I can't see her settling down to become Mother Earth.'

James grinned. 'I understand that. She's a

woman ahead of her time. There aren't too many like her around who are happy to survive without a man in their lives.' He paused for a moment. 'Don't get me wrong, I believe she loves you, old fellow. It's just from what I know of her and she's had it tough since her first marriage before marrying his lordship even, that she's a survivor.'

'And don't I ruddy well know it,' said Harry, shaking his head. 'I think though that's what attracted me to her in the first place. When I was on the verge of becoming engaged to Annabelle, I felt stifled, smothered almost. It was as if I was losing a part of myself as the woman made demands upon me. She'd have taken my very soul if I'd allowed it, but it's not like that with Cassandra,' he said wistfully.

'Then how is it?'

'For a start, she's not needy at all. She doesn't make demands upon me. None whatsoever.'

'That's a rare feeling indeed.'

'It really is. It's hard to explain but she completes me as a man.' Feeling an overwhelming surge of love for her he glanced at James. 'Would you mind ever so much if we cut this short? I've enjoyed our acquaintance and the fact we will be sealing the deal as far as the pit is concerned and I do look forward to working with you, but I need to go home. I don't like to leave my wife too long as her pregnancy is so advanced, though she's not due for a couple of more weeks.'

James nodded and smiled. Then he stretched his

arm across the table to shake Harry's hand. 'No problem. We can do this again. Perhaps we can wet the babies' heads!' He grinned. 'I'll summon the waiter to fetch the coachman, he's having a snooze in the snug area.'

Harry smiled gratefully realising that this time he could say, 'Home James and don't spare the horses!'

***

Cassandra was going through yet another contraction as she felt her abdomen tighten and she began to perspire profusely. The pains were getting harder to cope with and judging by the look of concern on Polly's face as she knelt beside her on the rug taking her hand as she squeezed and yelled out in pain, the woman was becoming very anxious indeed. A thought suddenly occurred to her. 'Emily!' she shouted out.

'Don't go worrying about Emily right now,' Polly said sharply.

'B...but I'm supposed to be picking her up from school this afternoon.'

Polly frowned as if this was one extra thing she could do without right now. It wasn't enough that the woman was having to deliver not one but two babies all on her own and there wasn't anyone around to help or even call for a doctor but now she had the added burden of worrying about Emily too. As if fighting to think carefully she said reassuringly, 'Look, when no one shows up to meet her, they won't send her home on her own. The staff there will realise something is up, after all, they all know you're heavily pregnant. Someone will either bring her home or she'll be taken to the Vicarage until someone can collect her. They're very good at the school.'

Cassandra forced a smile, realising that Polly was probably right. Then she felt an impulse she remembered all too well, that she wanted to push. 'S...something's happening,' she gulped.

Polly's eyes widened. She'd not had to deliver one baby before in her life never mind two but she had seen a midwife deliver her sister's baby a few years back. 'Are you feeling like you need to push?'

Cassandra nodded. 'Yes.'

'Then go ahead,' she said sounding more confident than she felt as she drew in closer towards Cassandra's bent knees. Then a couple of minutes later as Cassandra huffed and puffed, she yelled excitedly, 'I can see the head!'

It all seemed to happen so quickly as the baby's head which was covered in blood and mucous emerged and then a shoulder as somehow Polly eased that shoulder out and then another, until the baby had plopped out between its mother's legs. Part of the umbilical cord was still inside Cassandra along with the placenta, but the baby was born. Polly trembled all over as she wrapped the newborn in a blanket and handed the baby to its mother. Glancing at its nether regions she declared, 'It's a boy!' sounding as proud as punch. 'Hopefully, the other twin and the afterbirth will deliver soon.' And as she said so the baby let out an almighty cry and Polly handed him to his mother to suckle him. With tears streaming down her face, Cassie held him to her breast.

A sound startled them as the door opened and Harry came crashing through the door. 'Oh, my word. I'm so sorry I've been away when this has been going on.'

'There's not time for that,' said Polly shortly, casting him a glance. 'Go and fetch the doctor and see if you can get someone to pick up Emily. She's due out of school at any moment.'

Harry gazed lovingly at his wife. He knelt by her side and kissing her forehead said, 'I'll check to see if James's coach is still outside. If it is, as the coachman was attending to the horses when I came in here, I'll see if I can get him to take me to the doctor and I'll send word to my mother to fetch Emily from school.'

Cassandra nodded gratefully. Little had she known when she woke up full of beans that morning, feeling like she could clean the place from top to bottom that she'd end up going into labour. Everything felt upside down but now her husband was here, she felt reassured.

**

Fortunately for Harry, James's coach hadn't rushed off when he'd entered the cottage and there, in disbelief, he'd seen his wife lying on the floor in front of the fireplace with her newborn babe in her arms and Polly in attendance. But

'It's all right, Harry,' said Polly with tears streaming down her cheeks, 'the second boy has been born safe and well, though he's a lot smaller than his brother, he seems to be a fighter.' Then as if on cue, the newborn began to air his lungs as he cried with a high pitched yowl.

'Thank God,' said Harry with tears streaming down his face as he stood to embrace Polly. 'And my wife?'

'Cassie is doing well, though she's a little tired. I'm just about to make her and the doctor a cup of tea, would you like one?'

Harry nodded gratefully. 'Yes, please, I was about to make coffee, if you'd prefer that instead?'

Polly nodded. 'I'll make coffee for everyone else but for Cassie, I'll make a cup of tea as that's what she's asked for and she needs some rest after all the trauma of the day…'

A shot of guilt coursed through his veins. 'I didn't help I suppose, being gone for so long today when she needed me?'

'Now don't go blaming yourself, Harry, you weren't to know. These babies have made an early appearance.' Her eyebrows knitted together as if she was perplexed about something. 'But what happened to Emily, didn't you fetch her with you?'

'No, there was no time. The coach stopped off after picking up the doctor for me to ask my mother to fetch her from school, she's insisted on keeping her at Hawthorn Cottage until things have calmed down here.'

Polly nodded and smiled. 'That's a good idea. Now go through to see Cassie and the babies if you like. I've made her comfortable on the settee, propped her up with pillows and draped some warm blankets over her. Though later, we'll get her upstairs to her bed and those babies in their cribs, got them both in an old drawer from the dresser for now with some towels wrapped around them to keep them warm.'

'Thank you, Polly. Perhaps I'll carry Cassandra up the stairs just in case of any more blood loss?' he suggested.

'Ask Doctor Bryant about that, but it sounds a marvellous idea to me.'

Harry smiled and wearily wiped his brow, it was a long and trying day, to say the least, but the outcome was truly wonderful.

***

The following days were exhausting. Cassie needed her rest, so the babies were brought to her when they needed feeding or just a cuddle or soothing to sleep. Other than that, Polly took care of them, changing them and rocking them in her caring arms. Mostly she could pacify them both but sometimes they just needed their mother. Emily remained at Hawthorn Cottage during this time with Edna and Aunt Bertha, though the trio had been to visit a time or two and Emily was enthralled by her new baby brothers. Doctor Bryant had explained that the youngest was a lot smaller because the eldest had taken a lot of all you'll have to do is pop the roast in the oven and boil up the veg. I'll even send one of the girls over from the tea room with one of my special apple tarts.'

Cassie beamed. 'You are so good to me, you know. I don't know what I'd have done without you, Pol, this past few months since his lordship's death and even before that when you were Emily's nursemaid.'

'Oh go on with you now,' said Polly in a bashful manner as a scarlet flush spread across her cheeks. 'It'll do you the power of good to have one another's company for just an hour or two with no babies demanding to be fed or changed.'

Cassie nodded. It would be grand indeed to be able to talk to her husband in peace.

**

Cassie waited for Harry's return. He had told her that he'd gone to visit Jem and Clyde and would return home by four o'clock. The smell of the beef cooking in the oven range made her mouth water. There was a sugar sprinkled apple tart with a jug of cream awaiting in the pantry too. She'd made every effort to tidy up her appearance, washing herself in the old tin bath in front of the fire as soon as Polly had departed. A fresh pretty floral dress was selected from her wardrobe, and although she'd put on some pounds around her midriff since the twin pregnancy, she could still manage to get into the dress, even if it was a little snug in one or two places. She chose to wear her hair loose on her shoulders, tied with a pink satin ribbon on top which matched the roses of her dress. Pinching her cheeks so they looked fresh, she waited by the living room window for her husband's coach to return, but there was no sign of it. Frowning, she turned away in disappointment.

To be fair, Harry knew nothing of her plan so maybe something had arisen at the last moment.

***

Clyde was settling into an entirely different way of life at Hewitt Hall and hence, Harry had taken it upon himself as a former resident at the house to instruct his half-brother in certain social etiquette and how to deal with both the staff and callers to the house. Jem, of course, was living there to oversee things but Jem had told Harry he was concerned how Clyde was spending his inherited fortune of late, splashing it around as if it would last forever. And although Harry thought it inevitable to begin with, as Clyde wasn't used to dealing with a large amount of money, he felt it wise to speak to him today suggesting that instead, he invested most of it wisely with some allowance for luxuries and treats. The problem was that Clyde could be quite easily led at times, especially if he fell in with the wrong people and he was bound to now attract hangers-on and vultures who would pare him down to the bone if he allowed it.

***

A lump rose in Cassie's throat and she

swallowed hard. Lately, she'd been feeling thoroughly exhausted and was beginning to lose interest in things, even the tea room. She'd only managed to visit there the once since the twins were born and it had all seemed to be ticking along nicely without her, with Polly at the helm and Rose Barton and the new girl, Doris, working under her supervision—it was almost as though she wasn't needed any more. The only ones who really needed her were the twins who were hanging off her breasts all day and all night. Even Emily seemed happy with Edna, her new grandmother, fussing over her and she often chose to even spend the night at Hawthorn Cottage instead of returning home. But who could blame the child when all her mother's attention was spent on two bawling baby boys and her newfound father was busy elsewhere.

Finally, forty-five minutes later, when Cassie had almost given up hope of her husband ever returning at all, he arrived and asked the coach driver to wait a while, then he entered the house. He wasn't smiling though as he usually did, there was a look of severe concern etched over his face as his brow furrowed and his eyes darkened.

'W...what's the matter?' she asked as she stepped towards him. 'Is there something wrong with Clyde?'

He shook his head. 'No, he's doing quite nicely. I've asked him to curb his spending habits a little and have set up a meeting for him to see a financial advisor…'

'Then what is it?' All thoughts of the impending meal and relaxation time together for them both had flown out of the window.

'It's the men from Marshfield Coal Pit. I've just been sent a message to say there is some unrest there, so I have to go quickly.'

'But how do you know that?'

'A messenger was sent by James, he needs back up as soon as possible by the sound of it. Look, I'm sorry I'm going to have to go.' He held her briefly to him and placed a kiss on her forehead.

She watched him turn and leave and rush back to his coach and within moments he was on his way to the pit. She bit her lip, trying to keep the tears that threatened to form at bay. Harry hadn't even noticed that she'd made an effort with her appearance, especially for him, nor had he noticed the delicious odour of the beef slow roasting in the oven. What a complete waste of time. Now, what was she to do for the next couple of hours? She had them all to herself and no one to spend them with. She could give in and go back to bed for some rest but something told her not to do that. It would be like giving in as many times these days she felt like creeping beneath the covers and burying her head in the pillow. No, it was a nice afternoon for the time of the year, so, she'd put on her bonnet and cape and walk into Wakeford. Maybe she could call into the tea room and spoil herself with a cream bun and a cup of coffee. There'd be someone there

'It's like this...' began Tobias as Harry became aware of one or two men murmuring something behind him. 'That young lad, Benny Brewster, who died...'

'I know of him and his family,' said Harry.

'Well, us men have been talking and we don't want another Benny Brewster on our hands. There's lads working in this pit that are too young to go underground. It must no longer be allowed.'

'What sort of ages are you thinking of?'

'Those mainly under twelve years of age because that's now the legal age they're allowed to work since the act of 1860. '

Harry gulped. He had no idea that there were lads younger than that working at the pit. 'How old is the youngest?' he asked, noting that Tobias seemed to have calmed down now that he was being listened to.

'Seven, maybe eight-year-old.'

'I don't understand this,' said Harry. 'There was a law passed more than thirty years ago that forbade young children under the age of ten years old from working underground and women too.'

'Aye, another law was passed all right since the law previously which was only ten year olds allowed back then,' said Tobias. 'And you'll find no women folk working here, but some of the men have lied about their sons' ages. They've put them to work here to earn more for their families but it's not right.' He glanced around the crowd with a hard stare as if seeking out those men who had condemned their young sons, who after all were little more than babies, to a life of hardship.

'And what of the previous management here? Wasn't anyone aware of this?'

Tobias nodded slowly. 'Aye, they all were. They turned a blind eye because it suited them. No wonder your old man was so popular. He turned a blind eye himself to a lot of things, though in other respects he could be fair, mind you.'

Harry felt sick to the stomach. If there was something he could still pride himself on it was the fact that he'd felt at least his father had done things correctly at the pit but now, even that was a lie.

'I shall have a meeting with Mr Wilkinson and we shall come to some agreement about this. You have my word,' he said softly, shaking his head in disbelief. Tobias nodded gratefully at him. 'How many boys do you believe are really under twelve years old?'

'I should say about seven or eight,' said Tobias. 'Though one or two we're not really certain about as they might just be small for their ages.'

'I'm glad you have informed me of this. Rest easy,' he said laying his hand on the young man's shoulder. 'Conditions here are about to have a major overhaul...'

***

Cassandra pulled her cape from the peg on the back of the kitchen door and made her way out of the cottage and across the mountain pass at home that day either but she'd left a message asking him to call to the tea room, and fair play he had with a very fine offer for her to continue the business and Jem too, even if things had to change a little for them both. She drew in a deep breath and exhaled. There was nothing to fear now just a ghost of a memory.

To Cassie's surprise, Jem pulled the horse and cart up outside the house's main entrance and he whistled loudly until a stable lad arrived at his side and led both horse and cart away. 'You look startled?' he gazed at Cassie.

She smiled. 'It was just that I was expecting you to...'

'To hide both horse and cart out of plain sight of any snobby-nosed callers at the premises?'

'Something like that,' she shrugged.

He chuckled for a moment. 'We don't get many fine visitors here except for our auntie, or sometimes Polly or your Aunt Bertha. The only fancy guests we have calling here are usually after something, like bills what need paying and the like. That's why I needed Harry's help with regards to Clyde's finances, that lad needs reining in like my horse.'

Cassie quirked a brow. 'Are you that concerned then?'

'I'm afraid I am. Our Clyde went down to the village when he first moved into this place and he was splashing his money around like water, buying drinks for everyone and placing bets on all kinds of things and playing card games. It was evident if left to his own devices, he'd have no money left at all!'

'Then thank goodness he has you and Harry to look out for him, Jem.'

Jem lowered his voice. 'Did you know on one occasion he brought a large group of men back here late one night? Right nefarious sorts they were and all, it was obvious they were out for what they could get from him and I let them stay for a drink at first but when I caught one of them trying to pocket a silver teaspoon, I sent them all packing with a flea in their ears.'

'Who on earth were they? This is only a small village.'

He rubbed his chin. 'I've no idea, I only recognised one from The Ploughman's Arms called Jake McCarthy, the rest I'd never seen before in all my born days. I think word had got around about Clyde coming into a fortune and they came to Wakeford to find him. The daft beggar was easy to find an' all as he was spending a lot of time in the pub at that point. He's stopped his shenanigans now though, thankfully.'

'Thank heavens for that. It must cause a great deal of concern for you though, Jem.'

'Aye, it has an' all but with Harry's help and his contacts, we'll manage. You see, sometimes Clyde is like a man to all intents and purposes and other times, he needs treating like a child. That's for his own sake of course as he can be a right, Clyde. You should only be associating with trustworthy people right now.'

'Like who?' Clyde blinked.

'Well like us, Harry, Polly, Aunt Bertha and of course, Edna too. You know all of us and we're not after your money.'

'But I liked having friends, it made me feel good.' Clyde shook his head and for a moment Cassie feared he might cry but then he looked at her and said, 'I trust you, Cassie, and I know you wouldn't lie to me so don't worry I will be careful in future.'

Jem's eyes softened. 'No one's out to spoil your fun,' he said in a softer tone this time, 'we're just looking out for you that's all. You can and will enjoy your good fortune but you need to invest some of it, that's why Harry is arranging for you to see a financial advisor.'

Clyde nodded and then rose from his armchair. 'Please excuse me for a m...moment...'

Cassie began to rise herself to go after him as she feared he might be upset but Jem said, 'Don't worry yourself about him, he'll be back. He's often like this when he can't cope with something or another.'

'Thank goodness he has you, Jem,' she sighed heavily. 'Why doesn't he invest some of his money in your furniture business? Then you could have bigger premises, even a couple of shops around this area?'

Jem shook his head. 'Harry did suggest that at the beginning but I've built that business up from scratch. Maybe it's a pride thing but I want it to be my work not the money of William Hewitt behind it. He wasn't my father, he was Clyde's and I don't want the two worlds mixing if that makes sense?'

She nodded. It made perfect sense indeed.

cruel to her that Rose's father was now forcing them apart and that didn't sit right with her at all. Whenever Clyde became upset, she'd noticed his stammer got worse.

***

'The problem is,' stressed Harry, 'that most jobs beneath ground aren't without their particular dangers. The boys mostly work a long day often leaving home before six o'clock in the morning and remaining here until seven at night. They can be exhausted even before they arrive as it's a long trek for some. I remember my father telling me of a little girl, yes a girl, as they were allowed to work underground back in those days. She was only six-years-old. She was discovered sound asleep against a large stone underground. The poor mite's lamp had gone out as it had run out of oil. She was petrified and to top it all, someone had stolen her bread and cheese. Maybe it was the rodents or some crafty so and so who wanted to fill their own belly. Whatever, it shouldn't be happening to a child in the first place. You have a daughter of that age, James?'

He nodded. 'Yes, I do. Amelia, and she's so precious to me. I also have two older sons, Dominic and Gerald. They're aged nine and eleven years old.'

'Well, imagine then,' said Harry, 'your three young children, trudging for miles to even get up before daylight in all sorts of weather to get to the pit. Then spending around twelve hours in the darkness. One is a doorkeeper, operating the ventilation door allowing the coal carts through, another is on his hands and knees pulling the coal carts from the coal face and he's exhausted, and yet another is a driver leading the horses which pull the wagons along the main roadways. All three of your children are at risk of severe injury or even death, but you have to send them to work at the pit, need to as if you don't you can't feed all the mouths that need feeding back at home!' Harry said angrily, banging his fist on the desk as the vibrations travelled and caused a clatter as a pen and a metal letter opener clanged against the tin mug Arthur had left behind in his haste to depart the office for the men to talk.

James drew in a breath and released it again as he shook his head. 'You paint a dark picture there...' he admitted.

'And darker it will get if we don't do anything about it.'

'But what can we do if the boys' fathers, brothers and other relatives are fibbing about their ages? How can we tell the difference say between a boy of nine-years-old and one of eleven?'

'I admit that is difficult but I was thinking along a different line. If we could get the boys to do less dangerous work for part of the day and the remainder of the day, send them to school.'

James gulped. 'And how do you propose we do that?'

'By organising some sort of scholarship fund.

It's education that will pull those people out of poverty. If they can read and write and even in some cases, get as far as to university or even only in a position as a clerk in an office like Arthur who works here, then they will have an altogether better future.'

'I do understand your reasoning, old chap, but where is this money going to come from to pay for this?'

Harry hadn't thought this through as the thought had only occurred to him as he spoke and he'd verbalised it immediately to his counterpart.

'We'll sleep on it tonight and try to think of a way. My father was generous to the folk around here, particularly the widows and orphans of the parish and he gave money to the church to fund the school there. Maybe there's still some left sitting in a pot there ready for a use such as this.'

James blinked and shrugged, almost as though he doubted it, but it didn't deter Harry, for the first time in a long while he felt energised. He could do something positive for those boys, thankfully no girls were employed beneath ground these days, but anything he could do to help would placate those men, particularly Tobias Beckett.

***

It was almost nine o'clock when Cassie heard the front door of the cottage click open, she had fallen asleep in the armchair in front of the fire. Seeing Jem and Clyde once again had stirred up her spirit so much so that she made such a fuss of Gil and Ernie when Polly returned them later that afternoon and she welcomed Emily with open arms when Edna brought her home from school. Polly was surprised that the meal Cassie had planned hadn't as yet, been eaten, but she had commented on how the sparkle was now back in the young woman's eyes since going out that afternoon.

'Cassandra,' Harry said softly as he closed the door behind himself, approached and threw himself to his knees burying his face in her lap. Then looking up at her, said, 'Will you forgive me?'

'It wasn't exactly your fault you were called to the pit this afternoon,' she smiled. 'I was planning a special meal for us both so we could spend some time with one another but the good news is that it isn't ruined if you'd like it now? The children are all fast asleep upstairs so we shan't be disturbed.'

He smiled. 'No, I am sorry about that but I'm apologising for everything. I haven't been much of a husband to you lately. I've felt so out of things, not a part of anything since the twins' birth.'

'Believe it or not, Harry, that's how I feel too. I went for a walk after you left, over to the tea room, and peeked in the window there seeing it all ticking along nicely without me. I felt like crying but Jem spotted me and took me back to Hewitt Hall where I had tea with him and Clyde. It was so refreshing to get out of the house and speak with them both. Then Clyde brought me back home in his coach.'

'That was lovely for you,' he said, rising to his feet, then he drew her from the armchair into his arms. 'We must never lose sight of one another ever again...' he murmured softly.

Cassandra's breath hitched in her throat, it wasn't going to be easy when her husband had so much responsibility at the pit. Exhaling deeply, she whispered, 'No, we must never...'

**

And so it was arranged for a scholarship fund to be set up for the young working lads at the coal pit. Their work now involved lighter duties mainly above ground, apart from when extra help was required at the coal face and then they were allowed more breaks. There wasn't a pot of money as Harry had described it remaining at the church left by his father, just enough to keep the church school funded for another couple of years as money was used to fix the church roof and that had cost far more than the reverend had expected. But the man had taken great sympathy at the plight of the young colliers and had offered that some of them might attend the church school for four hours a day. He was able to take six of them and the other fourteen would need placing elsewhere. This was a real dilemma for Harry as he didn't want to leave any lad without educational instruction, all needed to be treated equally in his book. Then it came to him, an idea that he had been mulling around in the darkest recesses of his mind that he realised was coming to him in his dreams. A special school needed to be built for these lads for the future. He put the idea to James the following day when he visited him at Marshfield Manor.

'A school? Especially for the young colliers?' He stared at Harry as if the man had gone out of his mind. They were in the drawing-room and it was obvious to Harry that James had thought they were to have a snifter together as the brandy bottle was already out besides which were two clean crystal cut glass tumblers.

'Yes, that's exactly what I'm saying to you,' said Harry excitedly pacing in front of the long French window as James pondered what the man meant from the comfort of the winged armed chair by the side of the fire. He gripped the armrests as if somehow to ground himself.

'Surely you cannot be serious?' James blinked.

'I am and I've never been more serious in all my life. Think what it could do for this community to educate those young men, to give them more prospects in life?'

'I can see your point, but where is all this money going to be coming from?'

'I was just coming to that. I am prepared to sell my book shop to help fund it. I've discussed this with Cassandra and she's all for it though she did raise one good point and that's if the book shop is sold and someone opens it selling something else, then where else in this area will people have the opportunity to purchase a book and read? They'd have to go into Hocklea or Drisdale or even further afield. So...' he paused for a moment, trying to catch James's gaze. 'So, I was thinking that maybe you'd fund it with some of the inheritance from your father?'

James gulped. 'It's not as straightforward as all of that...' he said as if he'd been punched in the face by a twenty-stone heavyweight boxer.

'No? I think it's very straightforward. Your father did wrong by the workers at the pit. Don't you see that this might go some way to making amends? Come on now, you've inherited this beautiful house as your father purchased it after the lord's death and the coal pit itself, as well as some other businesses and properties. What would it be to you?'

James drew in a composing breath and let it out again. 'What you say is perfectly true but I have a wife to keep who has expensive tastes and two sons I'd like to put through the finest education system eventually at Oxford or Cambridge and, Amelia, who shall go to finishing school in Switzerland or Paris someday...'

'Yes, I can see all of that, but if you gave up a little of your newfound wealth you wouldn't just be helping three children like you are now, you'd be helping twenty young lads and those that come after them. Their families too if they can afford to pull themselves out of poverty sometime in the future by having a solid education.'

'Let me think about it,' said James. 'It's not

something I can give an easy answer to overnight.'

Harry nodded and took the armchair opposite his friend and colleague. 'Promise me you'll give it some serious consideration? I really think it will help a lot and give you good standing not just with the men, boys and their families but generally within the community...'

James nodded as he stared into the flames of the fire. Although summer was on the horizon, it was a bitterly cold day.

***

'So, you don't think James will do as you suggested?' Cassie asked her husband later that evening back at the cottage.

'I haven't a clue, to be honest, he's going to give himself time to mull over the proposition. But I was thinking, if he won't go for it, I'm prepared to give up the book shop as I mentioned and we have some savings as I've been saving up for a house for us...'

Cassie felt pained to hear him speak that way. 'I understand what you're saying,' she said approaching her husband and gently rubbing his forearm, 'but there must be another way that doesn't spoil our dream to have our own house someday.'

He turned his head in her direction and frowned. 'Is there though? If James doesn't dip his hands into his very long pockets, where else will this money come from?'

Suddenly, and without much thought, Cassie

murmured, 'Clyde...'

'What did you say?'

'Clyde!' said Cassie excitedly. 'I bet he would help you.'

Harry shook his head vehemently. 'Oh, I couldn't consider that. Our father left most of his fortune and Hewit Hall to him. We mustn't take it from him.'

'No, I wasn't thinking that way at all,' said Cassie. 'I was thinking more of a loan to acquire a property and one or two teachers. Maybe if you could interest local businessmen and they club together to come in on this scheme.'

'You mean like some sort of co-operative?'

She nodded eagerly. 'Exactly. Maybe it shouldn't be confined to just the boys at the coal pit either but those at the wool and cotton mills, anywhere where young labour is used.'

'Then that would have to include girls too in some cases?'

'Yes, of course.'

'Oh, I don't know this idea is running away now.'

'Think about it though, it would give those other businessmen and Clyde too some sort of status with the people of Wakeford and those from the surrounding areas.'

'Yes, maybe it would,' said Harry thoughtfully. His mind was working overtime now.

'If James won't stump up the cash for this, we ought to look around. The main thing required is a decent building for the school, the money to pay for some teaching staff and of course, food and drink for the children.'

'Cassandra, I could kiss you!' He drew her into his arms and brought his lips crashing down on hers, taking her breath away. And in that moment, there was no doubt of the love her husband felt for her and she for him, nothing or no one was going to get in their way.

Chapter Five

Cassie hovered outside the tea room. She'd timed it well as it appeared quiet of custom inside, she waited as the last remaining customer departed and then she entered. The little bell above the door jangled as it always had and Rose Barton turned to face her, while Doris stood at the counter wiping the crockery and putting it away for the day.

'Hello, Mrs Hewitt!' Rose said with a big beaming, welcoming smile, obviously pleased to see her employer. 'How are those babies of yours doing?'

'Hello,' Cassie greeted. 'Yes, they're fine, thank you—they're being minded by the other Mrs Hewitt at the moment, Edna, for me to pop in and see how you're both doing here. Would you come and take a seat with me?'

Rose nodded cautiously as a pink flush spread over her cheeks, it was at that moment Cassie realised the girl probably thought she was in trouble for something.

'Don't worry, Rose, you haven't done anything wrong, just take a seat, please?' Cassie drew out a chair from one of the tables for the girl to sit and then seated herself opposite her. Rose's eyes were shiny and bright and Cassie considered for a moment not to mention Clyde but then felt she had to. 'Clyde has been asking about you and told me to tell you he's thinking about you...'

'That's nice,' said Rose averting her gaze from Cassie's persistent one.

'He's told me that your father has stopped you from seeing him since he's come into an inheritance?'

Rose brought her gaze to meet with Cassie's. 'Sorry, Mrs Hewitt, that's not exactly true.' She began to fiddle with her hair and move around in her seat.

'Then what is true, Rose? You owe it to Clyde as the lad is sweet on you, surely you realise that?'

'I do, Mrs Hewitt, honestly I do.'

'Then what is it?'

'I...I've met someone, actually.' She swallowed hard.

'You mean some sort of beau?'

She nodded. 'We've been seeing one another since around the time Clyde first moved into Hewitt Hall.'

'I see,' said Cassie now smiling sympathetically. 'And you didn't like to hurt Clyde's feelings I suppose?'

'No. I like Clyde a lot but I never felt that way about him, I see him more as a friend than a beau. Then when he came into that fortune and moved into the big house, I never saw him around much and thought he'd forget all about me.'

'Well, he obviously hasn't,' said Cassie softly. 'The kindest thing would be if you would explain all of this to him next time you see him else he will get badly hurt if he sees the two of you together, or someone takes it upon themselves to inform him before you do.'

She nodded. 'I know you're right.'

'So that story about your father forbidding you to see him wasn't true I take it?'

'No, Mrs Hewitt. Not exactly anyhow. I don't think he sees Clyde as being good enough for me really deep down but he wouldn't have prevented me from seeing him if I wanted to.'

***

'At the heart of a boy's life in villages like here in Marshfield and neighbouring Wakeford, Drisdale and Hocklea, is the coal pit. He's raised within sight of it with coal dust in his nostrils and the sounds of the steam pump hissing in his ears. Since he was able to crawl on all fours, the child will have witnessed his father and brothers and other close family members, setting off for work at the crack of dawn. And then, the day finally arrives when the young lad has to set off for the pit too...' Tobias Beckett began to speak in front of the crowd at the pit entrance, his eyes bright with passion as he spoke with conviction. 'Indeed, the shadow of a pit such as this one here at Marshfield has dominated the landscape along with the cotton and wool mills and ironworks in this area and surrounding parts. The sounds of the clanging and the winding mechanisms are almost like music to their little ears. They feel the vibrations summoning them to join the other males in their families underground or in the case of the mills, they follow the females too. Children have suffered as a result. I don't have any children myself as I'm not married but I've heard tales of their suffering of fingers and even whole arms being lost at the cotton mill and the pit. Even young infants drugged up to the eyeballs on syrup of poppies for their mothers and fathers to work in such places while their infants sleep the sleep of the dead, and in some sad cases, those infants lives have expired by the time their parents return home! These are the days of industrial rule! Where earning a living wage is what folk want from these places but they don't want to see their own children suffer as a result of managerial negligence or unfair working practices!'

'I agree!' shouted a man in the crowd. 'I know of one man who used to carry his young son to work on his back in the mornings, this was going back a long time ago mind, but the poor mite was only seven-years-old and got so tired even before he began work at the pit. I know that doesn't happen these days so much but some of the boys in this pit are only nine or ten years old and their fathers are pretending they're twelve and older so they can get some work out of the poor blighters and more money in the family coffers. It ain't right!'

More of the workforce murmured in agreement,

but some remained silent as they knew they were doing wrong themselves. Tobias was about to say something else as he addressed the crowd when he noticed Harry and James draw near. He held his hand over his eyes to shield them from the afternoon sun as he glared in their direction.

'Now what have we here again?' Asked James sharply as the men's heads turned in his direction.

Harry, who tugged on his colleague's jacket sleeve to silence him, said, 'We have spoken at length about this issue and believe it or not, we are both on your side, gentlemen. We happen to agree with what Tobias has been trying to press home to you. Please listen to what we have to propose...'

Tobias stepped down from the wooden platform to allow Harry to take his place. He stood for a moment surveying the crowd before him. The bobbing heads of the men were mostly of those who wanted to see justice, he realised that. A fair day's work for a fair day's pay was their motto.

Tentatively, he searched for the right words to say. 'Yes,' he began, 'it's not right that young children, some who are underage of allowance by the law, are working here. We plan to put a stop to that immediately! That is the first thing I wish to say.'

'How?' Asked Tobias.

'Every child will either have to produce their birth certificate or else have a letter of proof from the local vicar or minister as proof of his baptism. It's the only way to make this fair.'

'And what if there is no proof?' Asked a man in the crowd who Harry recognised as Thomas Crowley. 'What if there is no birth certificate? That happens sometimes.'

'Then I think that will then be down to the discretion of the management,' James said with some authority. 'We will have the right to refuse a boy employment here if we believe he is under twelve years old as it's against the law.'

There was a lot of muttering and nodding of heads.

'What's the other thing or things you were about to say?' Tobias stared hard at Harry, his dark eyes glowing like two embers in the fire. The man was on fire himself with a passion Harry had not seen from their workforce before, this young man was hot-headed but then he had his principles too.

'I was going to say we have come up with a solution for the rest of the young boys allowed to work here. Their working day is to be slashed by one third!'

'A third? I don't know if I'd be happy with me son just earning two-thirds of what he's earning right now, mind you!' Shouted Thomas Crowley.

Harry shook his head. 'It's not as bad as it seems. They will be paid in full and their duties shall be a lot lighter; most will work above ground apart from those times when someone small is required to help crawl into difficult places et cetera. It's just that during the third of their normal working day they will be educated!'

'Educated? My son don't need no education!' Thomas yelled. 'I've managed well enough without it meself!'

'And that is why you're working somewhere like this,' snarled James as Harry cast him a glance. The last thing he wanted was to rile up the men.

'Although that is true to some extent,' Harry carried on, 'and yes, you've managed well without education, Thomas, can you read or write though?'

Thomas Crowley's face flushed red. 'No, not much at any rate. I can sign me own name as I was taught to do that but I can't do much else, I'll admit, but I'm a good worker here.'

'No one's disputing that,' Harry smiled. 'But wouldn't you want better for your son? If he gets educated then he will be able to read and write, he might even get as far as receiving a university education if someone sponsors him or he gains a scholarship. He might even obtain a job and earn a lot of money in a good profession, a lot more indeed than you're earning right now.'

Thomas grinned as if he was proud of his son already. 'I suppose it wouldn't do any harm and it will do the lads good to have a rest from underground for part of the day but what if we need them for something?'

'We'll arrange for them to go to school in shifts. Some will go from nine o'clock in the morning to one o'clock in the afternoon and others will attend the school from two o'clock until six o'clock on a rota basis to ensure fairness for all.'

'And just where will this school building magically appear from?' Tobias narrowed his gaze in Harry's direction.

'Eventually, we will purchase or build one that's suitable for purpose, but for time being some lads can use the church hall and I'm going to enquire around the area to see if any other churches or chapels will allow us to use their premises.'

Tobias sniffed loudly.

'Anything the matter, Beckett?' James glared at him.

Tobias lifted his head to make eye contact with his superior. 'Aye, there bloody is. I know what's coming next, you'll dock our wages to pay for this education.'

Harry smiled. 'Now that's an idea!' He said raising his index finger but then his voice took on a serious tone. 'No, we won't do that though I have heard of that sort of thing going on. I'm going to have a word with other businessmen in the area to see if we can form some sort of co-operative for all our young workers to receive four hours of education a day at a shared school.'

'Good luck with that!' said Tobias seeming unimpressed as he folded his arms. 'You'll not get nowhere as some of those bosses like at the cotton mill want to squeeze what they can out of those kids. They're not going to like allowing them off the premises for four hours a day and having to pay them when they're not there into the bargain!'

'Maybe he does have a point there,' James

whispered to Harry as Harry nodded.

'Yes, but we'll see. We can only try.'

James had a look on his face that seemed to say, 'I'm with Tobias on this one!' But pushing that mental image away, Harry carried on speaking to the men. When he had an idea in mind he wasn't one for giving up easily.

***

Harry stared at the satanic looking mill before him with its dark brickwork and tall chimney stack that seemed to dominate the landscape. It was the wool mill owned by the Fairley Brothers who were originally from up North in the Lancashire area, but their father had settled here when he'd hit on hard times and tried to begin all over again. He'd obviously made a success of it as lots of folk were employed here. Around the mill was a muddy stretch of water through which the workers trudged in to get to work.

Men, women and children toiled for up to sixteen hours a day here amid the deafening clamour of labour-saving machinery whilst the management sat in their offices or else inspected their workforce and ruled with a rod of iron. And all the while as they worked long hours they were sleep-deprived and at risk of enduring an industrial accident.

The stone floors echoed noisily as children dragged heavy wool in wicker baskets from one machine to the next for processing. A young girl of maybe eleven-years-old, stopped for a moment to rest. Harry felt like carrying the heavy basket for her to save her young back, but he realised he might get both himself and her into trouble if he did that. Instead, he smiled at the child, who did not smile back then he turned away and gazed around himself at the strands of dyed yarn that were strung from the iron nuts and bolts. It was a hive of activity.

Noticing a man who was smartly dressed as he addressed two of the workforce, he made his way in that direction. The man appeared to be some sort of manager or foreman.

Just as he reached him, the young woman and young lad walked away as if about to perform a special task for the man. 'Excuse me, sir,' said Harry.

The man looked at him with avid interest as he took in Harry's neat appearance, no doubt he could tell he was a man of means so he smiled. The same would not be true, Harry was certain, if someone of less standing had approached him.

'And what can I do for you?'

Harry cleared his throat, the air in here seemed claggy and he guessed it was to do with the wool fibres circulating in the air. 'I'm seeking Mr Fairley.'

'Old Mr Fairley or one of the sons?'

'Whichever one is running things around here, I suppose.'

'Then you want Anthony Fairley, he's the eldest son, the other two are Nicholas and Benjamin.'

'So the father isn't in charge anymore?'

him.'

'No, she didn't by the seem of it. She's a nice lass but I think she viewed him as a friend, obviously it was an affair of the heart for him.'

Harry glanced at the tea room window and then turning back asked, 'And who might this new beau be then? Anyone I know?'

'Aye, you ought to an' all.'

'Oh?' Harry quirked a curious eyebrow. 'How should I know?'

'He works at Marshfield Coal Pit. Name's Tobias Beckett!'

'Knock me down with a feather! That's the young man who has been speaking out recently, causing a bit of a stir with the men.'

'Doesn't surprise me. I chat to him often enough at The Ploughman's Arms, he's always fighting for some cause or another.'

'But he'd be a few years older than Rose?'

'Aye, yes he is. I think he's about twenty-three-years old. I can see though that Rose's father would welcome someone like him as Arthur Barton is a bit of a fight for your rights sort himself. Can't abhor the upper classes. Clyde thought at first that Arthur had warned her to stay away from him as he'd come into a bit of money, but seems from what she told him yesterday it had nothing to do with that.'

Harry shook his head. 'Poor Clyde. So where is he now?'

'Still in bed I should imagine and he won't be

getting up the rest of the day neither. Cook has been sending his meals up to him but he's barely touched them.'

'The lad is probably love-sick. It will take some time to get it out of his system. Meanwhile, is there any way I can help you cart any of this furniture inside?'

'Yes,' said Jem appreciatively.

'I'll just remove my jacket and leave it in the book shop then.' Harry returned a couple of minutes later with his shirt sleeves rolled up beneath his waistcoat. He spent the next ten minutes or so helping Jem cart the grandfather clock, a table and a cabinet up the stairs to the emporium. Both men then sat to catch their breath.

'How's it going at the pit then?' Jem asked.

'There was trouble afoot regarding some of the colliers' sons being too young to work underground but that's sorted now and we're hoping to open a school so they can be educated for four hours a day in shifts.' Jem raised a brow of surprise. 'Not just children from the pit but we're thinking of forming some sort of co-operative whereby children from the mills can join in, that's if the mill owners' can be persuaded.'

'That sounds a good idea to me. As you know I've recently learned to read and write myself and what a difference that has made to me! Now I don't feel left out and foolish and I can read books about antiques and discover more. There's a whole world didn't usually allow strangers into their home but this man was no stranger to either her husband or Rose.

***

Tobias took a seat at the table as Cassie busied herself brewing up more tea. She emptied the old leaves from the teapot into a small bowl. She never threw them away, either she dried them out or put them in the garden around the roses to help them to grow well. Although she'd once had a more affluent life as Lord Bellingham's wife she still knew the art of being thrifty, it was seared into her soul as she also knew what poverty was.

She poured the water from the boiling kettle on the hob into the awaiting teapot which contained fresh tea leaves and put on the lid, turning to glance at Tobias she blushed as she realised he'd been watching her the whole time. Why was he having this effect on her? There was something so disarming about him in general she realised. Nothing bland about this bloke.

Forcing a smile to cover up her awkwardness, she carried the tea tray to the table and set it down taking a seat opposite him. 'I'm afraid I haven't baked today, haven't had time to with the twins. But there's a slice of sponge cake left over that's still fresh if you fancy it?'

He nodded eagerly as she passed it to him on a china plate. Greedily, he took it in his coal-grained hands, taking great big bites and swallowing quickly.

'Good grief!' she said with some surprise. 'Haven't you eaten today yet?'

'I have, yes,' he said between mouthfuls as she quickly began to pour him a cup of tea so that he might wash the cake down. He paused for a moment as he swallowed. 'I don't know what you must think of me and my manners but it was early this morning when I last ate.'

'Don't you stop for a break underground to eat your food from your snap tin?'

'Aye, I do of course. We all do. The bosses encourage us to eat, fair play. But this morning there was a little lad new to the shift, only twelve-years-old. At least he is the required age to work underground not like some we've had working for us, but I'm pleased to know that is coming to an end. No more underage lads in the pits is a good thing.'

She nodded. 'Sugar?'

He waved his hand. 'No, I'm sweet enough,' he chuckled. Then his face took on a grave expression. 'Anyhow, as I was saying, this young lad, Bartie Gates, he came to work for his first shift and had left his snap tin at home. Poor little blighter. He were scared of being in the dark and all so I told him I'd look after him and share my food with him. I'd taken some bread and cheese along with me and an apple but when I saw how thin and puny he looked, I kind of felt sorry for the lad and ended up giving him most of mine.'

A surge of admiration arose unexpectedly inside

Cassie. 'Why, that's most kind of you. So you went without for that young boy?'

He nodded with tears in his eyes. 'Oh, don't make me out to be some kind of hero though, Missus Hewitt, I can't afford to give him my food every day but I might pack a bit of extra in case he forgets his snap tin again.'

'You mean you don't think he really forgot it?'

'No, I don't. Seen it happen afore. Some families are so poor they might give their son a bit of bread to eat or some oatmeal before setting out and that's if they're lucky. I think they hope the benevolence of the colliers working with their son will feed him.'

'I see,' said Cassie gravely. 'Now then, as you've gone without and are obviously starving, how about I make you something a little more substantial?'

'I don't want to put you to any trouble though?' He frowned.

'No, it's no trouble. You did a kind act today. How about some bacon and eggs?'

Tobias nodded eagerly. Cassie took her cup of tea with her whilst she set the pan on the hob to fry. It was something hot she could prepare quickly for Tobias with some bread and butter. There were plenty of eggs in the larder and bacon too. It was no hardship for her. After all, there were plenty worse off than herself.

When Tobias had finished and mopped up the last of the fried egg from his plate, he sat there with a satisfied grin rubbing his stomach. 'Thank you so much, Mrs Hewitt. Eggs and bacon never tasted so good.'

She'd enjoyed watching him eat with relish. 'What was it you called about?' She said finally. She hadn't felt like asking when the man was so hungry.

'It was you I wanted to see, actually.'

'Me?' What could he possibly want to see her about?

'It's Anthony Fairley, the eldest brother, at the wool mill. Your husband went to see him a couple of days ago with regards to setting up this co-operative to build a school for the child workers.'

Cassie nodded with some understanding. 'Yes, he did but he told me he didn't get very far with him?'

'From my understanding, Mr Fairley gave your husband short shrift and showed him the door.'

'Oh,' her hands flew to her face. 'I didn't realise it was as bad as that. Harry gave me the impression that he'd just called at a bad time and negotiations would be ongoing.'

Tobias shook his head. 'No, the door was firmly closed in Mr Hewitt's face. I know a little more about it see.'

'How?' Cassie angled her head to one side.

'One of my mates, Angus Deacon, works at the mill and he heard it all, he was stood outside Mr Fairley's door when Mr Hewitt was asked to leave.' Tobias paused for a moment. 'So, I was wondering...' His face reddened. 'If you, Mrs Hewitt, would approach the man instead.'

'Me?' She felt perplexed. 'But why would Mr Fairley listen to a woman?'

'Not any woman, you! He'd respect you as he was good friends with Lord Bellingham.'

'I'd almost forgotten that,' she said with honesty. 'Yes, of course. I knew him a long time ago. I only ever encountered him a few times. I was just introduced to him and his wife and he seemed most formidable. Then he called to the house now and again but eventually, he stayed away as Oliver got into debt. But what can I do that my husband has failed to do?'

'Speak to him about what is good for those children and how it will benefit the mill if they have rest and education, please?'

Cassie could see there was a fire in the man's eyes. He wanted this more than anything else and although she realised, Tobias was considered a bad lot by some in the area, she could sense he had a lot of good in him too.

Chewing on her bottom lip, she said, 'I can understand your reasoning behind this but I doubt if what I have to say will have any bearing on matters...' She was being honest as since moving into the village of Wakeford she had fought a hard battle to be accepted into the village. 'To be truthful, it's taken some time for the people here to even accept me as one of their own.'

He nodded. 'I quite understand that but that

makes you an even better prospect to get through to Anthony Fairley in my book. You were up against it settling here in the first place but look at all you have achieved. Aye, I heard the rumours but you won folk over in the end, didn't you?' He gazed into her eyes.

'I...I suppose you are right,' she admitted. 'But why are you so invested in this?'

His young face became etched with worry lines as he continued, 'Because my younger brothers and sisters work at the wool mill, Mrs Hewitt. I want them to be able to better themselves.' He took his cap from the table and began to twist it between his hands almost as though he were wringing someone's neck as he said, 'Those bosses at the various mills around here will squeeze dry from the kids any drop of juice they can get from them. Oh, they don't mind that they work long hours for little pay or might lose a finger or even an arm from the machinery at the mill!' He raised his voice causing Cassie to startle as his dark eyes flashed passionately.

'How old are your siblings?' She asked softly, wishing to calm him down.

He became grounded once again as he lowered his voice and set his cap back down on the table. 'The youngest is ten-years-old. He shouldn't be working there under the age of twelve anyhow, but my mother is widowed you see, and our Sam, well he lied about his age to help her out. I wasn't happy about it, but his heart is in the right place.

Then there's Tess who is twelve-years-old, Simon who is thirteen, Tilly is fifteen and the eldest, apart from myself, of course, is seventeen, his name's Peter. I worry about them so much but at least they all have employment and our Ma has their wages coming in.' Cassie nodded, seeing his predicament. 'Is it a crime to want better things for them and other children in the area, Mrs Hewitt?'

'No, it is not,' said Cassie firmly. 'I shall think it over and discuss it with my husband tonight if that's all right with you?'

He smiled as though relieved and was about to say something else when there was a cry followed by another coming from upstairs.

'Right on cue,' she smiled. 'I'll have to feed them and change them.' She was assuming he would get up and leave but instead, he looked at her.

'How about I make you a cup of tea while you do all of that? Yours went cold I expect whilst you made me that food.'

Surprised she raised a brow. 'That's very kind of you. Would you give me ten minutes or so though to sort the boys out before brewing up?'

He nodded. 'Sure. I'll have a nice cup of tea waiting for you on your return,' he said his eyes sparking with energy and vitality.

Upstairs, shakily, she soothed the crying boys. She didn't know what to make of the young man downstairs in her kitchen. It was so unusual for any man to offer to make her a cup of tea. But then again, Tobias wasn't just any man, was he? He was someone who clearly cared about others.

***

Harry was in a good mood as he whistled walking up the path towards the cottage. It had been an interesting afternoon helping Jem out at the furniture emporium. Jem, these days, was like his confidante and his unofficial adopted brother. They'd spoken about all sorts of things though Clyde, naturally, was at the top of the list as both brothers cared deeply for him.

As he entered through the front door of the cottage he heard voices, it sounded as if Cassie was entertaining someone. It was a man's voice he heard quite clearly chatting easily with her. For a moment, he couldn't quite place it but as he drew nearer he recognised the voice of Tobias Beckett. No wonder he hadn't recognised it at first as the man was speaking in a soft, easy manner and making all sorts of silly noises at the boys. Feeling a little uneasy, he removed his coat and bowler hat and hung them on the hall stand.

The kitchen door was ajar and what a merry little scene he saw before him, the door frame was like a picture frame of happiness he observed. Tobias was making silly faces at Gilbert and Ernest was being rocked back and forth. Indeed, they all looked like a family he was no part of. But what did the man want here?

As he entered, he noticed their empty teacups on the table and glanced at Cassie who smiled at him. 'Hello Harry,' she said. 'We have a visitor.'

the cake mixture with a wooden spoon.

As if realising she was being watched by the both of them, Polly stopped what she was doing to catch Cassie's eye. 'Aye, me an' all. Now don't misunderstand me, when I first met Edna I thought she was so high and mighty, like you did I expect, Cassie?' Cassie nodded. 'But now I've got to know her properly and have heard her story, I understand why she was the way she was being married to that William Hewitt. The men at the coal pit can laud his name all day long, but he treated his wife appallingly in my book.'

'I don't think he was as fantastic as all that,' said Cassie shaking her head.

'Why do you say so, Cassie?' Aunt Bertha peered over the top of her spectacles in her niece's direction.

'Because Harry has heard gossip from the men at the pit and it looks as if his father turned a blind eye to children working below the legal age underground. They were also made to work longer hours than they should have been.'

Polly gasped. 'I bleedin' knew that halo of his had to slip at some time or another.'

'Harry said to me that he thinks the reason his father went back into the pit that time to try to rescue Benny Brewster was that he thought the lad was underage working at the pit. Turned out he wasn't anyhow and both perished in that explosion, but if William had survived and that boy was found to be underage he would have got a right ticking off for it. Might even have ended up in prison.'

Aunt Bertha gasped.

'So,' said Polly pushing the mixing bowl to one side and resting her floury hands on the table, 'it's a no wonder Harry is so keen to make amends at the pit.'

'Yes,' sighed Cassandra. 'James Wilkinson too for his father's past demeanours.' She became reflective for a moment.

'Are you daydreaming there, Cassie?' Polly asked as Aunt Bertha studied her niece over the top of her glasses.

The truth was she had been thinking of her encounter with Tobias Beckett and reflecting on what a remarkable young man he was. She was surprised when she'd returned downstairs that afternoon that he'd left without saying goodbye to her. Then something occurred to her, had Harry sent him away? If so, why was he reluctant to have the young man around? It was almost as though he was jealous of him. Jolting back to reality, she laughed. 'You know what I'm like Pol when I start thinking about things.'

'What were you thinking of?' Polly arched an eyebrow.

Before Cassie had an opportunity to answer there was the sound of voices and Emily burst into the kitchen, closely followed by Edna. Emily approached Cassie as she sat at the table and wrapped her arms around her mother's neck.

'Have you had a good day, poppet?' Cassie smiled as she hugged her daughter closely, relieved there would now be no further questioning from Polly.

'Yes, Mama,' said Emily drawing away and looking up at her mother. 'We did sums and spelling at school and I got everything right so Miss Adams called me to the front of the class and gave me an apple!' She said proudly.

'Well done, Emily!' Her mother smiled.

'And Granny Edna has just shown me some of her ballgowns!' Emily declared enthusiastically as Edna beamed behind her.

'I was just thinking...' Edna said clasping her hands, 'that I could cut most of my gowns down to make a few party dresses for Emily. After all, I won't be needing them anymore.'

'That sounds a splendid idea, Edna,' Polly approved. 'Though keep one or two for special occasions as you never know.'

'Thank you that would be most kind of you,' Cassie beamed.

Emily stood back and looking at Polly asked, 'When will that cake be ready to eat, Auntie Polly?'

Polly chuckled and said, 'Not for some time, but I'm just about to scoop it all out of the bowl into the baking tin. How would you like to lick out the bowl for me so I don't need to wash it?' She winked at Cassie.

'Yes, please!' Emily glanced back at her mother. 'If I may, Mama?'

'Yes, of course,' said Cassie. 'Then we'll have to

set off home. Rose Barton is babysitting for me, so I don't want to leave her too long.'

'Very wise an' all,' said Polly approvingly. 'She's a good gal but her head's in the clouds since she got involved with that Tobias Beckett!'

'Oh, he's not so bad,' Cassie said, leaping to his defence. 'He called around to the cottage to discuss some pit business the other day.'

'Quite a headstrong young man by all accounts!' Aunt Bertha pursed her lips. 'They were discussing him in the post office the other day.'

'Why were people talking about him, Aunt Bertha?' Cassie frowned.

'I didn't get all the gist of the conversation as it was mid-flow when I entered but apparently, he's fighting for the men's rights underground.'

Cassie nodded. 'Yes. But it's more than that. He wants to help the young children too. There are many children working in these parts not just in the pit but at the wool and cotton mills too who are doing so illegally.'

'Whatever do you mean?' asked Edna.

'They're not of legal age but their parents are pretending they are. As a result, they are working overly long hours in dangerous conditions.'

'I see,' Edna sniffed. 'How is it that never seemed to happen when William was pit manager?'

'Oh it did, believe me,' Cassie carried on as she watched Emily licking the cake mixture in the bowl from her fingers, all the while so glad she didn't have to send her out to work.

Edna quirked a puzzled brow. 'But I never got that impression it went on. All appeared above-board.'

'There was a lot that was hidden back then according to Harry.' Cassie angled her head to one side as if in sympathy for those young souls.

'That's terrible!' yelled Edna, causing Emily to startle. 'Sorry,' she apologised. 'I'm still angry about how William treated me but I'd always got the impression he was well thought of by the men.'

'He was,' said Cassie. 'They knew no better either really, just did as they were told. After all, if a father had just moved to the area and said his son was such and such an age, who could question it?'

'If you ask me,' said Polly, 'no child should have to work. Not until they're at least fourteen.'

Everyone nodded as all eyes were on Emily, whose face reddened as she realised she was being watched. But those were empathetic eyes for the welfare of the little girl and Cassie realised that her daughter and sons, thankfully, would have better lives than those who went underground or worked at the mills at such a young age.

**

Tobias and Rose were out walking on the mountainside. It was a Sunday afternoon and they tended to enjoy their walks together. There was hardly a cloud in the cerulean blue sky. Birds chirped noisily in the trees and a warm breeze ruffled their hair. Tobias took Rose's hand in his own and drew her towards him to plant a kiss on her lips, but instantly she drew away from him, startled.

'What's the matter, pet?' he asked looking into her eyes.

'My Pa says I got to stay a good girl till I'm wed,' she said.

He smiled. 'But one kiss won't hurt, will it? And who's to know? No one can see us up here?' So far all he'd ever got to do was hold her hand and kiss her cheek and sometimes hold her close to him, so he could feel her body close to his. The swell of her breasts against his hard, firm chest. It was no longer enough for him though, at his age he needed more.

'I...I don't know if I should,' she said, her voice trembling now.

'It's all right', he smiled, 'I'll take you home.'

'But I thought we'd come for a nice walk?' She looked confused now as her vivid green eyes blinked, but he was bored with her company anyhow, she didn't have much to say for herself. All she talked about was working at the tea room and how she was sewing herself a new dress. What the material was like, where she'd bought it. Now, Cassie Hewitt, there was a woman who had much to say and she was interesting too. Although several years older than him, he felt strongly attracted towards her. That evening after visiting her at the cottage, he'd found himself obsessed by her, she consumed his waking thoughts.

'All right, I'll let you kiss me then,' Rose said

suddenly as if she feared losing him. She lowered her eyelids in a demure fashion. He smiled and drew her close to him, his heartbeat thudding in his ears as he brought his lips crashing down on hers. He closed his eyes, in his mind he was kissing Cassie, tasting the sweetness of her rosebud shaped lips and embracing her womanhood, inhaling her sweet perfumed skin. She was indeed, every inch a woman and thinking of her aroused him even further.

Rose yielded to him as though enjoying his passionate embrace, so he thought he'd try going a little further as now, after all, this was Cassie and not Rose anymore, but as his hand crept up inside her skirts, she slapped it firmly away. He realised she was playing the long game here. Oh, she'd give in eventually, but not today. They always did in the end as they wanted to play it all virginal and sweet for some time not for him to believe they were of easy virtue and for the most part, they were not, they just needed some gentle, persistent persuasion. A kiss would be enough for today and a bit of flattery. Next time he might get as far as fondling Rose's breasts. But he wanted to make love right now as his mental image of Cassie had whipped him up into a frenzy of passionate feeling. He realised he couldn't take Rose by force even though he had half a mind to but if he did, there'd be her father to contend with and he respected that man who would probably force him to marry his daughter if that occurred. He was going to have to find someone of easy virtue meanwhile to give him what he wanted. He was a man with needs after all. The person who came to mind was May Malone, she'd probably be plying her wares at The Ploughman's Arms again or if not, he'd call around to her house and ask to take her out somewhere. Her family didn't much care what she got up to as long as she brought the money in. They were a poor lot since arriving from Ireland, so every farthing counted to them.

'Come on then,' he said taking Rose's hand, 'I'll walk you back home. There's something I've just remembered that I need to attend to.'

Rose's face took on a look of confusion as she frowned. For her, she'd just experienced the most passionate kiss of her life, Clyde had never kissed her that way, only a peck on the cheek and once on the lips. Now it was all over and Tobias was taking her home. Still, he must really like her to kiss her like that she thought and whatever she did right now she needed to keep him at bay until they were wed or her father would have her guts for garters!

***

Cassandra and Harry had made an appointment to speak with Anthony Fairley at the wool mill. They were seated in the man's office as a young woman was dispatched to make them all a pot of coffee. Cassandra gazed around herself as she shifted around in her hardback chair as she imagined workers might be called into this room to be reprimanded on occasion, spying a bottle of whisky on his large mahogany desk, she guessed all kinds of business deals and decisions were made here too. The office looked quite imposing with its long floor to ceiling oak bookcases, marble mantlepiece fireplace and dark furnishings. It was a far cry from the frenzy of activity on the floor beneath which echoed with whirs and clanks as the sounds from the carding machines which separated the dirt from the woollen fleeces and the rattling from the spinning machines, seemed in perpetual motion. Water power was utilised to drive the heavy machinery, the mechanised mill turned fleeces into high-quality yarn which was sometimes exported overseas. It was a veritable hub of activity at the mill.

Anthony Fairley was stood near the window with his back to them, rubbing his chin as if in contemplation. Dropping his hands to his sides and turning, he spoke. 'I didn't realise you were Cassandra's husband when you called here recently?' He stared hard at Harry.

Harry smiled. 'I...I didn't think to bring it into the conversation.'

'No, and why would you?' Cassandra frowned. 'Look, the truth is Anthony, you were a close friend of the Lord's and he admired you so much.' She knew she was flattering the man's self-image, but if that's what it took to get him to listen to what they had to say then so be it.

Anthony Fairley nodded slowly. 'But don't you both understand that if I were to allow each child here four hours from their shift a day to get educated, I'd lose a large chunk of my workforce? Besides, I think some of their parents would be opposed to this co-operative scheme you suggest as they'll fear losing valuable funds that are coming in to supplement the household.'

'It doesn't need to be like that though,' Cassandra said gently. 'If four hours is too much to be taken from their working day, then how about two hours instead? Any education would be better than none at all. It will give their little bodies a rest that they badly need, and as a result, there might be fewer accidents in the workplace.' She could see she had got through to him as if he hadn't considered that. 'You wouldn't lose all your workforce in one go either as we plan on operating a shift system. Half the children educated in the morning, the other half in the afternoon.'

Anthony Fairley turned his back on the pair once again as he stared out of the window down onto the cobbled path below where workers were pushing trolleys of wool for washing and spinning towards the building. They'd just had a delivery from one of the farms in the area. He remained silent for a moment causing Harry and Cassandra to exchange glances with one another. Then he slowly turned and looking at them said, 'I think we could try this on a trial basis. I'm not promising anything mind you as if production goes right down then I'll stop it altogether—the mill can't afford to lose money or too much of its workforce.'

Cassandra beamed. 'You won't regret this,' she said. Although she sounded confident, she was concerned that the scheme might not work but she knew they had to try so that children in the area could have a better future.

After shaking hands with the man, Anthony holding on to Cassandra's hand a little too long for her liking, they chatted amicably over a cup of coffee. Though from time-to-time, Cassandra noticed Anthony shot some appraising glances in her direction and she hoped her husband hadn't caught those in case he called the deal off. The truth was, even back in the days when she was married to Lord Bellingham, she'd been aware that Anthony Fairley had a liking for her and for that reason, she ensured she was never left alone with the man. But, here, today had been fine with her husband at her side. What could the man do to her?

Harry and Cassandra travelled back home in their coach but as they were halfway there, Cassandra noticed Harry's face clouding over.

'What's wrong?' she frowned.

He shook his head and tapped the heel of his hand to his forehead. 'I clean forgot.'

'Forgot what?'

'The men at the pit were due to have a meeting this morning. It went right out of my mind, I thought it was tomorrow.'

It was so unlike Harry to forget something like that, he was usually so sharp but she had realised that he'd taken on a lot with running the pit and his bookstore in Wakeford. Whilst it was just the retailing of books, he'd seemed more relaxed, but now there were additional pressures added on. She realised he was just adapting and the bookstore itself might no longer present enough of a challenge for him.

'What time did it start?'

'It hasn't yet. It's due to start in twenty minutes, but by the time the coach drops you off, dear, and I get to the pit, it will be halfway over.'

'Then I shall come with you!' Cassandra said determinedly. 'Rose won't mind babysitting for an hour or so longer. I hadn't specified a time for our return.'

Harry visibly relaxed and then he took her gloved hand and held it to his lips before saying, 'You are the sweetest wife imaginable but the pit is no place for a lady. You'll have to either remain in the coach or take a seat in the office.'

She nodded. 'I don't mind staying in the coach,' she said briskly.

'Very well, just this once and I promise to keep on top of things in the future. What a day this has been so far, I couldn't believe it when Mr Fairley caved in like that. It must have been your power of persuasion, my dear.'

Cassandra smiled, realising it was more than that. Anthony Fairley had always admired her and had hinted on more than one occasion in the past that he was envious that Oliver Bellingham had got there first as he'd nudged her husband with his elbow and winked, but then the man's face had taken on a more serious expression behind Oliver's back and she'd realised he'd meant what he'd said. She wasn't about to tell Harry that little nugget of information though, but maybe his fondness for her would come in useful again sometime in the future.

***

When they arrived at the pit the men were gathered around as James stood on a wooden platform. Cassandra's eyes scanned the crowd to see if there was any sign of Tobias, but there was none. She wondered if perhaps he was working a different shift today. It would be unlike him to miss a meeting from what he'd previously told her of his passion to fight for his rights and those of others.

Harry's face took on an anxious expression. 'Looks like something's afoot,' he said as the coach driver pulled up beside the crowd. 'Wait here, if you will.'

She nodded and then watched him open the coach door, disembark and close it behind himself to join the men, striding purposefully towards them. There was a lot of murmuring and nodding of heads from the crowd as he arrived on the scene. Cassandra opened the coach window to see if she could hear what was being said. The men seemed oblivious of her being present, it was almost as though she was an unseen observer.

'Now men,' James Wilkinson was saying firmly, 'I thought we'd already reached an agreement about this!'

'No, we haven't!' shouted a man from the back of the crowd. Initially, it was hard to tell how old the man was but as he walked towards where James stood, as the crowd parted to allow him access, she could tell he was a middle-aged man.

'Why do you say that?' James Wilkinson asked.

'Because it's still not right. We need more frequent checks underground after what happened that time with the last explosion. The men had been reporting for a couple of weeks about the smell of gas underground. Your father did damn all about it though!' He spat on the ground as if in disgust and the men jeered. 'And now since the last mine act of 1860 was passed we have the right to appoint our own pit inspector!'

The men raised their fists in agreement as a collective shout abounded.

James Wilkinson's face reddened. He was looking most uncomfortable, Cassandra thought. Then she noticed Tobias, he was there after all. He looked up at James on the platform and requested he should speak, James nodded as he got down to allow Tobias the platform and the audience.

'All right, men. Calm down, please!' Tobias said with some authority. 'It's most unfair of you to blame Mr Wilkinson for the sins of his father.' Some of the men nodded and murmured in agreement. 'What I'm suggesting is this...'

Cassandra was astonished at how a young man like Tobias could rally the troops together and get them to take notice of what he was saying. It was mesmerising to observe. '...that we give Mr Wilkinson and Mr Hewitt time to sort things out and arrange to appoint an inspector here, if that doesn't work, then fair enough, we'll appoint one ourselves. They have only both recently taken over from their fathers and need to be given a fair chance while they find their feet. Mr Wilkinson senior, we know that a lot of you are angry with, but he's no longer here for you to vent your frustration at. His son though is trying to make amends. William Hewitt, on the other hand, was popular but let me tell you, and you might not like to hear this, but he too had his faults...' he shot a glance at Harry who visibly squirmed and put his palm to his face. Realising just how Harry felt towards his father, Cassandra sympathised with him. Was Tobias about to rub salt into an already overexposed wound? But then he said, 'No, he wasn't perfect, he made mistakes too from time to time but he was well-respected and you men cooperated with him and he did try to help you. You knew you could go to him if you ever had a problem.'

One man nodded. 'Aye, that's perfectly true,' he said.

'Yes, I went to him on many occasions,' said another.

'Good then,' said Tobias. 'Now you need to go

to either Mr Wilkinson or Mr Hewitt if you have any concerns. They are doing their best here to keep Marshfield Coal Pit going to secure all our jobs. Mr Wilkinson could have sold this on to some unscrupulous person, washing his hands of our employment at this pit and then where would we be?' He threw up both his hands expressively as if tossing something in the air.

'Yes, I suppose you're right,' agreed another man.

'Believe me, I am,' Tobias continued. 'From now on we work with the management, not against them! We do it to feed ourselves and our families. We do a fair day's work for a fair day's pay!'

A big roar went up from the crowd. Tobias had evidently dissolved what might have been a nasty situation for both her husband and James Wilkinson. Cassandra's admiration for Tobias grew even more.

Chapter Eight

A few days later Cassandra and Harry consulted Alfred Middleton, the owner of the cotton mill, who was surprised that his contemporary, Anthony Fairley, had joined the co-operative and encouraged by this, he decided to sign up too. For time being, the church hall was used on a rota basis to teach the children. Cassie became involved herself there with a couple of the other helpers from the original church school, all the while, suitable premises were being sought as a permanent fixture for the new school. Help came from an unlikely sauce in the guise of Mrs Lizzie Butterworth who had inherited the property in Wakeford known as The Grange House from Harry's father. The property was much too large for her, besides, she had the guest house to run, so she was more than happy to rent it out for the time being to the co-operative on the proviso if all worked out with the running of the school that the co-operative would purchase it themselves within the year.

Permanent teaching staff were sought and interviews held there to select the right people. Finally, a schoolmaster from Drisdale called, Mr

Newton, was appointed along with two male school teachers and one female. Cassie felt it imperative that a female should be appointed too as she wanted to give women the chance many never had as they were often looked down upon in society and the males made to be more important than they were. As a woman herself, she realised that women often had as much to offer as their counterparts and maybe sometimes even more.

Within weeks, the school was up and running and things were also ticking along nicely at the pit. Regular inspections were made underground, the men had received a small pay rise, the boys were being educated and now no lad underage was allowed to work underground. If the management was in doubt, a birth certificate or some other proof was required such as a record of baptism or something similar. Failing that, a doctor would be appointed to weigh and measure the child to approximate his age. The same was happening at the mills too.

The only thing that now troubled Cassie was the fact that so much of their money was being invested into this scheme that she wondered how they would ever afford a home of their own. The roof over their heads belonged by rights to Jem and Clyde and although both were happy they remain there for time being, Cassie did not intend to take advantage of the situation and neither did her husband.

One evening, Harry drew her to him and said,

'I'm sorry I can no longer afford to spoil you, I'd love to buy you a new gown or something like that,' he said looking at the same old dress she'd been wearing for months. She owned a couple of day dresses and one for best but she also had some posh ballgowns hanging up in the wardrobe from her days as Lady of the Manor. 'It's all right,' she smiled at her husband. 'I've been thinking things through and I've decided to sell the wooden carved beechwood bureau, most of my ball gowns and the silver set of cutlery I was allowed to keep after the Lord's death. After all, what use are they to me now?'

'But you love that bureau, and the clothing and silver cutlery might come in handy when we entertain in our new home someday.'

'But that day is a long way off,' she protested. 'We have to live in the here and now. They might fetch a good price. I expect Jem might buy the bureau and cutlery set to sell on and there's a shop in Hocklea that takes expensive ballgowns to sell to the public.'

Harry nodded slowly probably realising that once Cassandra made up her mind about something she was unlikely to change it.

'So be it then,' he said solemnly.

The look of guilt on his face caused her to frown. 'Now don't go taking the blame for this, Harry. One day we'll have our own home but for time being we have to cut our cloth accordingly,' she said and then she smiled and hugged him. 'For time being, we're doing the right thing to improve conditions at the pit for the boys and men and at the local mills too.'

'I suppose you're right, Cassandra,' Harry conceded. 'I just want to give you the finer things in life.'

'There'll be plenty of time for that later. Now how about we both have an early night as it's a big day tomorrow for The Grange House School.' It would be the first official opening day and a dignitary from London would be arriving to cut the red ribbon and someone from *The Wakeford and District Times* would be covering the story too. It would be a proud moment indeed.

He nodded and draping an arm around her shoulder drew her near to him for a kiss. It was some time since they'd been intimate with one another and tonight would be no different as to acquire enough sleep they'd need to go upstairs right now before the twins woke up at some ungodly hour again.

***

Rose was peering through the tea room window and as she noticed Clyde making his way to the furniture emporium, she paused to wave but he appeared not to notice her. It had seemed an age since she'd let him down and she'd not seen him since. She'd got the impression from Polly that he'd been heartbroken when she'd informed him about her feelings for Tobias. On the weekend they were due to meet up again for another walk. Slowly over the weeks she'd been allowing Tobias to take liberties with her but they hadn't gone as far as actually making love, but the way it was going it would prove difficult to cool his ardour. Part of her liked teasing and tempting him and she'd enjoyed their little fumbling sessions as she'd realised what she'd been doing couldn't make her pregnant but it did give her pleasure. Now she wondered if she allowed him to go further with her if she did indeed become pregnant that he'd have to marry her then as he respected her father and he wouldn't allow him to get away with despoiling his precious daughter. She began to hatch a plan so that the inevitable would eventually happen, even though it was obvious he'd been holding back from the actual deed. Now it seemed that she was the one in charge and not him.

Still, it would have been nice to remain friends with Clyde but she guessed that was no longer possible.

'Hurry up, girl!' Polly scolded breaking into her thoughts. 'You're as much use as a wet dishcloth there! What's the matter with you? There's tables that need clearing. Set to it!' She clapped her hands together, startling Rose.

Doris glanced at her and frowned.

'You too, Doris. Shirkers don't get paid in this establishment. Now Mrs Hewitt is busy helping at the new school, and it's a very big day there tomorrow, I need you both on your toes as I don't know for sure if she will ever return here to work.

So while the cat's away, I'm in charge!'

Both girls exchanged glances. Yes, it would be nice Rose thought if Tobias had to marry her, then she'd have some status around here and wouldn't be treated like a silly young girl any longer.

When the girls had cleared the tables and orders taken, there was time for them to chat for a while as Polly excused herself to use the outside privy. 'What is the matter with you today?' Doris looked into Rose's eyes.

Rose felt her face flush and she blinked. 'Just thinking about someone that's all!'

'Clyde?'

'No, not him. I was thinking about Tobias and how we might *do it* this weekend.'

Doris's mouth gaped open. 'Oh, Rose, you mustn't do that. Not until you're married. Look what happened to my sister, Frannie. She gave in like that, got herself in the family way and now Ma and Pa have an extra mouth to feed after her so-called fiancé fled.'

'Where did Frannie's fella flee to?'

'I think he joined the army and was fighting overseas. This was a couple of years ago. There is talk though that he was spotted in Hocklea fairly recently and although my sister has tried to find him there, so far she's failed. Don't go making the same mistake she did.'

'I won't,' said Rose as her chin jutted out. 'No fear. If I go too far with Tobias he'll have my father to answer to. He won't leave me like that.'

Doris nodded slowly but it was evident by the look in her eyes that she didn't believe what Rose was saying for a second.

***

The following day Cassie was setting out one of the schoolrooms at The Grange House for the day ahead. Chalkboards were placed on each desk along with fresh pieces of chalk. A colourful globe took prominence near the blackboard by the window and adjacent to that was a large imposing desk for the teacher. The esteemed visitor was due soon from London. Mr Barclay Fitz-Warrington was a London lawyer who had associations with the Wilkinson family and was a good associate to know regarding setting up the new school for the young colliers and mill workers. He knew and understood the law inside out. Today, he and his lady wife, Millicent, would be cutting the red ribbon to announce the school as officially opened.

Polly had been up baking all night and a selection of miniature sandwiches, pastries and cakes were set out on a long table in the assembly room next door. The room was in essence two large rooms knocked into one and nicely decorated so that when the children needed religious instruction or gathering together then this would be the room used. Rose Barton and Doris had brought over several teapots from the tea room and tables and chairs were set out with lace table cloths for the dignitaries and the press.

All was set to go as Cassie awaited the arrival

of the children who were to wait patiently at their desks. She glanced at the wall clock to see that its hands had seemed to take an age to move, there was still a quarter of an hour due for their arrival and all was ready. She heard the murmur of voices in the assembly room as Polly and her helpers were still laying out the spread.

There was a knock on the classroom door and she could see through the half glass structure, the face of Tobias Beckett. Cassie's heart began to race, why was she feeling this way? A frisson of excitement coursed through her veins as she blushed. She smiled nervously at him as she made her way to the door. Opening it, she looked up at him.

'Sorry if I've disturbed you at a bad time,' Tobias was saying with his flat cap in his hand.

'That's all right. I've a few minutes yet until anyone arrives.'

'I just wanted to thank you and your husband for talking to the mill owners. My brothers and sisters are right excited about coming to school today.' He smiled a beaming smile that lit up his face. Mostly, he had an intense expression etched on his face as though he had the weight of the world upon his shoulders but when he smiled like that, Cassie noticed, it took years off him. He really was a handsome young man. He'd also obviously made an effort to spruce himself up. His face and hands looked very clean. His long dark hair was slicked back from his face and he must have been wearing his Sunday best as his jacket and shirt looked quite new.

'Come in,' she welcomed as he entered the room and looked all around himself.

'My word this looks the business this new school.'

'You approve then?'

He nodded slowly. 'Aye, I do.'

'You'll be wanting to stay then for the opening ceremony?'

His dark eyes looked uncertain for a moment. 'Is that allowed when those knobs show up?'

'Yes, it's to be at my discretion. There will be a few villagers present such as Doctor Bryant and some shopkeepers and the like.'

'But I'm not as noteworthy as what they are!' He protested.

'Look,' she said, guiding him further into the room, 'you'll be my guest. After all, it was your idea that kicked this whole thing off. In fact, I'd like you to say a few words, if you will?'

His eyes flashed with passion. 'Aye, I could do, couldn't I? Will the mill owners be here an' all and your husband and Mr Wilkinson?'

She nodded. 'Say your piece about the place and what it means for the boys working underground to come here and your siblings of course at the wool and cotton mills.'

He beamed. 'Don't worry, I won't go on too long —I'll just say enough to provoke a reaction.'

Oh, he was good at doing that all right, she

realised.

'Yes, that's exactly what I'd like you to do. I'm sorry I never thought of it before. I don't want anyone else laying claim to what was originally your idea. Some are good at that trying to claim the credit for someone else's hard graft.'

He nodded. 'Aye, I know what you mean, Mrs Hewitt.' He was looking shy now as he gazed down at his boots. Those looked newish and all and highly polished to a shine. Maybe if he'd cut his hair he'd pass as someone from a better class, not like one of the mill masters of course, but he could pass for a shopkeeper maybe or a clerk. It was a shame she thought that he'd dedicated himself to a life of toil and torment underground when he was clearly an intelligent young man.

'Can you read and write, Tobias?' she asked.

'Aye, I can. Enough to get by anyhow. I write my name and read some books as long as they don't have too many words in them.'

'Splendid,' she said smiling. 'If you'd ever like me to tutor you and introduce you to the works of great fiction and non-fiction too, let me know as you know my husband owns a book shop.'

'I had heard about that though I've never set foot inside.'

'Oh you must,' she implored. 'There is nothing like knowledge from books to help you succeed in life. Now you take Jem Clement as an example. He owns the furniture emporium. He couldn't read or write when I first met him. He took classes at the church hall. Now he's reading books about antiques and all sorts and it's helping him with his business.'

Tobias's eyes darkened for a moment. 'I know him from the pub, but I don't know if reading would help me much underground though, it's a physical job for sure.'

'Yes, it is, Tobias. But think about what knowledge could do for you. You'd be able to read books and check up on laws relating to the pit, find out more about politics and policing, the list is endless. You could really stick up for your rights then.'

He rubbed his chin. 'Aye, you're right.'

'Think about it as I'd be quite willing to teach you.'

He smiled and as he did so she felt her body tremble with desire for him. What was she doing here? She had no more mind to think of it as the door opened and Polly walked in looking surprised to see the two of them together.

'It's all set out nicely next door,' she said, then sniffing cocked her head at Tobias. 'Hello, Mr Beckett.'

He nodded back at her. 'Good morning,' he said, obviously not knowing her name.

'Thank you, Polly. You may return to open the tea room now. Am I able to keep Rose or Doris here to serve tea?'

'Yes, just the one, mind you, as I have a feeling we are going to be rushed off our feet at the tea room otherwise.'

Cassie was just about to suggest she keep Rose to serve up when she noticed the look of uncertainty on Tobias's face. 'You take Rose with you then, Polly. We'll manage fine with Doris and if she needs any help, then I'll step in to give her a hand.' She glanced to her left where she noticed Tobias exhaling as if relieved that climbing, clinging Rose would not be hanging around his neck. Now he could relax for a while.

'Very well,' Polly agreed. 'I'll see you later.' Then stepping forward she touched Cassie's shoulder with affection. 'Good luck today,' she whispered in her ear.

Cassie nodded and hoped with Tobias at her side, she was not going to need it.

***

The opening ceremony went ahead promptly on time with the pupils seated at their desks as Mr and Mrs Fitz-Warrington swept into the place almost as though they were royalty meeting with their subjects. Barclay Fitz-Warrington was a tall, good looking man. His silver-grey hair at his temples gave him a distinguished appearance and Milicent struck an imposing, elegant figure as she glided into the classroom. She was tall for a lady but held herself so well that she reminded Cassie of the models she had once seen displaying ballgowns in Paris when Oliver had taken her there on their honeymoon.

After a guided tour around the school where

the Fitz-Warringtons got to meet the staff and view all the classrooms, they were led to the assembly room, where several speakers were set to say a few words before morning tea. Harry and James both spoke collectively to the room, each complementing one another's remarks. That was well received and there were several rounds of appreciative applause afterwards for them. Even the mill owners, Anthony Fairley and Alfred Middleton said a few words though neither was so forthcoming as James and Harry. The problem was Cassie thought that both still had doubts this scheme would work and might affect their businesses badly. James and Harry, on the other hand, had no such doubts, they wanted what was best for their workforce even if it came at a cost.

Harry was just about to rise to the podium to tell everyone that morning tea was now being served when Cassandra grabbed hold of his arm. 'There's someone else I'd like to hear speak,' she said firmly.

Harry raised an enquiring brow. 'Who on earth?'

'Tobias Beckett!' She nodded in the direction where he was sat at the far end of the room at a table to himself. Evidently, Harry hadn't noticed him until now and he looked perplexed for a moment.

Gathering his thoughts he said, 'I don't know if this is a good idea. Who knows what that young man might say, he's so headstrong.'

'Look,' Cassandra lowered her voice and through gritted teeth said, 'that young man was good enough to save your bacon the other day. If it hadn't been for him there might have been a revolt on your hands. Half your workers might have walked out of the pit, he calmed the situation down. Now I've had a word with him and he won't say too much, but it was his idea after all, not yours really.'

Harry let out a long breath as if admitting defeat. She was right of course. 'Very well,' he said with a scowl on his face, 'but if he ruins this for us then he shall never get a chance to speak about it again and his job at the pit will be in jeopardy.'

She nodded and smiled, then touching his arm, more gently this time, said, 'You'll not regret it.'

'I hope not,' Harry whispered beneath his breath.

True to his word, Tobias went to speak to the crowd as the local journalist from *The Wakeford and District Times* wrote fast and furiously to take down what was being said, by his side sat an artist who was taking likenesses of all the speakers as they spoke.

Tobias began, 'Ladies and gentlemen, thank you for allowing me to speak here today. It's long since been my vocation since working at Marshfield Coal Pit to have a platform such as this to pitch my speech regarding children working in heavy industry. As many of you know, for years now, young children, both boys and girls have worked underground in coal pits, on factory floors, up chimneys and the like until certain laws were passed at Parliament forbidding certain age groups to do this. Back in my father and grandfather's days even children as young as six-years-old were doing dangerous jobs and all for a pittance.' Cassie noticed Tobias's eyes flashing dangerously as they often did when he spoke with great passion and she feared for a moment he was about to say something he shouldn't, but she let out a sigh of relief as he carried on. 'But now we are seeing more responsible pit owners such as Mr Wilkinson and Mr Hewitt here today who have taken over from their fathers and forefathers and even the mill owners like Mr Fairley and Mr Middleton are now taking an interest in the welfare of their staff at the mills by ensuring the child workers there get an education and a bellyful of food. It's my understanding from Mrs Cassandra Hewitt,' he smiled at her from the podium, 'that each child as well as being provided with several hours of education here a week where they will leave their jobs at the pit or mills, will also receive a good meal to fill their empty stomachs. Some of them come from families so poor that they may have empty bellies all day but now thanks to the benevolence of these good men, changes are afoot and I commend it wholeheartedly. I work at the Marshfield Coal Pit myself and my brothers and sisters work at the mills, so I, for one, am pleased about this!' He nodded towards all four men who either smiled or returned his nod as a mark of respect as the audience began to clap and cheer.

Cassie was relieved that Tobias had kept what he wanted to say brief. He had said things there without implicating anyone whilst lavishing praise on the masters. He was a clever, articulate man indeed. Even Harry was beaming broadly as the journalist was now asking him questions in front of the audience. Finally, Harry took to the stage to thank everyone and to inform them refreshment would now be served. The morning was a great success.

Chapter Nine

Clyde was just emerging from The Furniture Emporium when he almost collided with Polly and Rose who were about to enter the tea room. It was well over a month since Rose had called at Hewitt Hall to give him the bad news about herself and Tobias. As if not knowing how to react, Rose's face coloured up and Polly noticing this said, 'Here's the key, girl, get along inside with you as we have to open up soon. I just want a word with Clyde here.'

With her head down with shame, Rose took the key from Polly's outstretched palm. Polly watched the girl fumble with the key in the lock for a time until finally, she got herself inside. Turning towards Clyde, Polly said, 'I've not seen you for a while around here, lad. You keeping all right?'

Clyde smiled at her and nodded slowly. 'I suppose you know what happened with me and R…Rose?'

'Aye, I do and I can't say I'm holding with it meself. What she wants to go off with someone like Tobias Beckett for I'll never know. She needs someone steady like you. He's a rabble-rouser in my book!' She stuck out her chin as if in defiance. Polly had noticed though that Cassie spoke highly of the young man and seemed to hold him in high esteem but she'd also noticed that Harry didn't hold with him either. He just seemed to tolerate him and kept him sweet so he didn't whip up any further trouble at the pit.

'It's a…all right, Miss Polly,' Clyde said kindly. 'I am feeling a lot better now. I have accepted that Rose's heart is with another and there's nothing I can do about it. I just wish her well that's all and hope that given time we can be friends once again.'

Polly smiled and patted his arm. 'That's the spirit, son! Now I know you won't want to call into the tea room any time soon, not when she's around at least, but I'll send up some nice custard slices upstairs later for you and your brother! I know how much you like those!'

Clyde's eyes lit up. 'That's most kind of you, Miss Polly.'

'I'll leave you to it then, Clyde. I've got a busy day today. Been over to The Grange House School as it's the first official opening day. Doris is still over there serving up.'

He nodded. 'See you later,' he said as he headed towards the horse and cart with his hands in his pockets.

Polly shook her head as she watched him go. That Rose one had really taken a large piece of Clyde's heart with her when she left him for someone else. The girl was just not the same anymore. Her head seemed in the clouds. She was in love, of course, Polly recognised that but what she had for Tobias seemed bordering on some magnificent obsession, it just wasn't healthy in Polly's book.

***

Everyone had left The Grange School, the morning had gone tremendously well. Cassie was about to lock the main door and head off to Edna's cottage to pick up the boys. The woman had recently moved into her new home and was settling in nicely there. Hearing someone cough, Cassie turned, surprised to see Anthony Fairley standing behind her.

'Oh, I thought you'd be long gone!' she blinked several times.

He smiled. 'I was. The coach was halfway up the hill when I realised I'd left my walking cane behind. I wouldn't have minded so much but it's my best one and worth a bob or two.'

'Where did you leave it?'

'In the headmaster's office, I think. I was last in there speaking to him.'

'Ah, Mr Newton's room. I'll just see if I can find it for you, you'd better come with me.' She opened the main door and they walked along the corridor, their voices echoing against the walls. The chat was lively and upbeat. Cassie pushed open the door of the headmaster's room where she spotted the cane standing in the corner.

'Ah, you are correct. Here it is.' By the time she had bent over to pick it up and turned around to face him, Anthony Fairley had already closed the space between them and it was making her feel most uncomfortable as she was cornered like a hare set upon by a pack of hounds.

'H...here it is,' she said nervously, hoping he'd take a step back but when he failed to do so and she noticed the look of lust in his eyes, she said, 'my husband will be back shortly he's just popped over to the book shop.'

'No, he hasn't, my dear. Why are you telling fibs?' he chuckled as if he was taking some great pleasure in this. 'Your husband has returned to Marshfield Coal Pit. I heard him speaking with James Wilkinson. Seems there's business there that needs sorting out and there's business here that needs sorting out too. I know you've always wanted me as much as I've wanted you.'

Cassie's voice caught in her throat as fear flittered through her body. 'No! That's just not true. I've never felt that way about you.'

'Come here, I've always thought you a tease. That's how you managed to snare Oliver while his wife lay on her death bed as you enticed him with your charms. You were hardly a maiden when you met him either, so you knew what it was all about.' He roughly grabbed her, causing the cane to fall from her hand with a clatter on the floor as he pulled her tightly into his arms so she couldn't get away. Her heart began to beat wildly and she felt as though she'd die from the very fear that consumed her. To her horror, he clamped his mouth over hers so that she wasn't able to protest, leaving his hands free to roam up her skirts. They were clawing now, dragging and yanking to get her drawers down. His intent was evident. This was all about to happen so quickly and she was powerless to resist as he was much stronger than herself. She closed her eyes to prepare herself for the worst. Her mind was detaching itself from her body.

Somewhere in the distance, she thought she heard the door click open and footsteps but how could that be as she was still being held fast. Then she heard a man's voice yell, 'Unhand her, you brute!'

Cassie's eyes flicked open and she noticed Tobias stood there, his face full of anger and fury as his mouth was set in a grim line and his eyes seemed to enlarge. Caught in the act, Anthony Fairley wasn't quite sure how to react. 'The Trollop enticed me!' He yelled and she's getting what she's after!' He brought his hands to his sides as Cassie's skirts fell back into place.

Looking directly at her, Tobias said, 'Tell me with your own lips that you didn't want this man's attention, Mrs Hewitt?'

It was obvious by the tears in her eyes and the way she was trembling all over, the man's advances were unwarranted, nor did she like any of it, but it was evident that Anthony Fairley needed to hear this. 'N...no,' Cassie stammered. 'He came back for his walking cane and accosted me while I was returning it to him.'

'As I thought,' said Tobias. 'Let's fight this out

like men!'

The whites of Fairley's eyes were on show as though he feared the young man. 'Don't be soft, you'd come off worse, not because I'm physically stronger than you but because I can pack a punch in other ways through the courts.'

'How about if me and Mrs Hewitt were to go to the police about this attempted rape for that is what it is?'

'Is that what it looks like to you?' Fairley smirked. 'Then I would lie and say you both made it up. I can afford to employ the best lawyers and you'd end up in prison and losing your job.'

'But I bet you can't afford to chance that, Mr Fairley, can you?' said Tobias as he spat out the words as if he were spitting orange pips onto the pavement. 'I might lose my job and my liberty, but you'd lose your reputation and possibly your family too if it came to that! And even your family's reputation. Maybe the mill would go under too!'

As if realising the sense of that, he glared at Tobias. 'Then how can I buy your silence?'

***

'It's quite simple, Mr Fairley...' Tobias said, all the while glaring the man in the eye. 'To buy our silence you have to do our bidding. Whatever Mrs Hewitt wants, Mrs Hewitt gets or else her husband and the law will hear of this.' He glanced at Cassie for her approval and watched her nod at him.

'Very well,' Anthony Fairley said sombrely,

realising he had lost the war for his reputation was at stake here and his own marriage and family business. 'You can name your price,' he stared hard at Cassie causing her to tremble again. 'But it's a one-time only offer. I'll only make it this once. I can't be held over a barrel forever.'

Cassie swallowed hard. 'I'll accept your offer but only on the basis that you never come near me when you're alone ever again.'

He nodded slowly. 'You have my word.'

'Then you have my word that I won't go to the police about this.'

'Or your husband?' He arched an uncertain brow.

'Nor my husband either.'

'Then we have a deal,' he said as he made to walk away from the pair, brushing past Tobias. Tobias grabbed a hold of the man's arm and dragged him back. As if fearing the worst, Fairley yelled. 'Hey, I thought we have a deal?'

'We do. You just forgot this, that's all!' Tobias said handing the man the expensive-looking walking cane. 'We wouldn't want your wife wondering what happened to it now, would we?'

Fairley scowled and grabbing his cane from Tobias's grasp strode out of the room. Tobias went to the front door of the building to watch he'd gone for good and firmly bolted it, then he returned to Cassie's side where quite naturally, he took her into his arms. She felt safe and protected as he held her and softly he stroked her hair and planted a kiss on top of her head. 'Are you sure you don't want to contact the police?' he asked. 'Never mind what was said to Fairley, if you want to I'm quite willing to take you and tell them what I was just a witness to?'

'No,' slowly she shook her head and gulped back the tears. 'No, I just want to forget all about it. Thankfully you arrived when you did. He owes me a big favour now, one he can never get out of as we both know something about him that he wouldn't want others to know.'

'Yes,' Tobias nodded gravely allowing her to move from his embrace as he looked deep within her eyes. 'And he wouldn't want your husband knowing either nor the rest of the villagers. Men like him make me sick!' Then as if realising she needed comforting for longer, and spotting a bottle of brandy on the headmaster's desk, he offered to pour a glass each, which she gladly agreed to. There was no way that she wanted to rush over to Edna's in this state. The man had made her feel grubby inside and out, it was as if he had soiled her in some way, even though he hadn't actually had sexual relations with her it was enough that he'd tried to kiss her forcefully and his hands had roamed where they shouldn't have.

'I'll be forever grateful to you, Tobias,' Cassie said as she wiped the tears away with the back of her hand.

He nodded. 'You don't owe me a thing though,' he said. 'I'm just happy to be in your company, Mrs

Hewitt.'

'Cassie, please,' she reiterated.

He nodded and smiled. 'Cassie.'

A frisson of desire crept over her, and feeling silly about having such an emotion, she whispered, 'You'd best pour that brandy, I need it.'

'Me too,' he smiled and winked as he caressed her tear-stained cheek.

***

That night in bed, Cassie tossed and turned so much that she decided to get up and sleep downstairs not to disturb Harry. As she rose from the bed with her pillow tucked beneath her arm, she watched the rise and fall of his chest—he was sleeping peacefully, totally unaware of the earlier fracas at the school when everyone had departed. For him, it was a successful day, a good day indeed, but for her, it had turned into a nightmare. It wasn't just the awful ordeal with Anthony Fairley that upset her it was the fact that she was developing feelings for Tobias who in some ways had now become some sort of protector towards her. She wondered if it was Harry who had discovered what happened earlier how he would have handled the situation. Would he have faced up to the man quite boldly like Tobias had, putting him in his place and turning a bad situation around to her advantage? Yet, she felt maybe not as her husband had already cowed down to the man when he'd first approached him, alone, to ask if he'd become part of the co-operative. That particular time he'd been sent away with a flea in his ear.

It was past three in the morning when she finally fell asleep in the armchair near the fireplace with the pillow beneath her head as she lay with it on the arm of the chair with the rest of her body curled up and her woollen shawl draped over her form. It wasn't ideal but at least she managed three hours of sleep before the twins awoke. They were later rousing this morning which suited her so she could grab that extra hours sleep, three hours rest wasn't enough for anyone to make it through the day. She was just going to have to grab another hour later in the day even if she couldn't sleep she could rest. Today, she had to return to the school to help out. It was only meant to be for a week or two while all the staff settled in and she was a floating member of staff, required where necessary. She wondered though how she was going to feel walking into the headmaster's office after what had occurred yesterday?

She pulled herself up from the armchair rubbing her stiff neck. She must have slept awkwardly, then she stoked the fire which thankfully was still in and banked it up with lumps of coal. Then she put the kettle on to boil before fetching the twins. Although she could hear them upstairs, neither one was crying to wake Harry up otherwise the fire and kettle would have had to wait.

Edna would be arriving at around eight o'clock to mind the twins. Today she was staying at

It was only arranged for her to work there for a few weeks until all the staff and pupils settled in there. Then she'd be free to either return to being a full-time mother once again or if she wished, to take over running the tea room and Polly would step into her shoes. He wasn't the sort of husband to quash his wife's hopes and dreams, far from it. Before leaving for the pit, he decided he'd have a word with her after work when he returned home that evening.

Tobias had surprised him with his speech to everyone on the school's opening day, he seemed to have impressed a lot of people, particularly the editor of the local newspaper who had made it the lead story on the front cover of *The Wakeford and District Times* the following day. The article garnered a lot of interest and focused its attention primarily on Tobias rather than the mill masters and the colliery owners. Though the article did display them all in a good light, describing them as "Modern thinking, benevolent sorts of masters who genuinely had the best interests of their workforce at heart." which was all thanks to the words Tobias had spoken of course. It was clear there was much more to this young man than Harry or indeed, anyone else had ever thought. He decided to call him into the office later to thank him for his kind words which it was obvious that the young man had chosen carefully to hammer his point across and at the same time stress what was needed for the children who were risking life and limb by working in heavy industry in the area.

Later that morning at the pit, it was evident that James was in high spirits as he slapped Harry amicably on the back. 'I have to say, old bean, that opening ceremony at the school was a complete success, especially since Tobias, the man of the people, had something to say!'

Harry nodded slowly. 'Yes, I was thinking the same thing myself and maybe he ought to be rewarded in some sort of manner.'

'You mean to keep him sweet?'

'Good heavens, no, man. I mean for speaking with such candour, and of course, for averting possible trouble at the pit the other day too.'

James rubbed his chin. 'Are you thinking of a pay rise as all the men have recently just received one and I don't think they'd like it if he received more payment than them for the same work?'

'No, not that. I was thinking of promoting him.'

'Oh!' said James, his eyes widening with surprise as if it was something he hadn't considered at all. 'To what position may I ask?'

'Foreman.'

'But Tom Langstone has been doing that job for as long as I remember here. I used to visit here as a child when my father had this place, he was here then. Think he's been here both man and boy from the very beginning.'

'Exactly. He's too old for the job now and still traumatised after that explosion, don't think he'll ever get over that young Benny Brewster's death nor my father's either.' James nodded sombrely as Harry continued. 'Needs a younger man with a bit of mettle to do it. Tom's only doing half a job.' He sighed loudly. 'If Tobias takes over as underground foreman, he'll be subordinate to the manager. He can set the pit to work each morning and attend to all the detail of arranging the work and getting the coals each man works to the shaft bottom. It will also be his duty to see that each working place is properly ventilated thus increasing safety measures. I understand from my wife that he can both read and write so he should be able to keep written accounts and he can keep an eye on the men for us at the same time.'

James arched an interested eyebrow. 'So, Tobias would also be our eyes and ears underground and would be our channel between us and the colliers?'

'If you'd like to put it that way, then yes, but he'll be accountable to Sykes in the first instance, the manager.' Sykes had been appointed since the death of Harry's father. 'The attraction of the job for Tobias, as well as having more responsibility, will be the extra money he'd be able to bring in.'

James thumped Harry heavily on the back as if pleased with the concept. 'You're not just a pretty face, my friend!'

Harry regained his composure after the hefty whack and grinned. No, he certainly wasn't, but would Tobias go for the idea that was the question?

***

'No, Mr Hewitt, I'm sorry I can't do it. The men would hate me for it!' Tobias was standing in the pit office facing Harry and James across the desk, shaking his head vigorously. He stood with his cap in his hand as a mark of respect for both men.

'But what makes you say that?' James looked up at him.

'They'd probably view me as someone to lord it up over them if I accepted the situation. As it stands, I am still one of them and can help fight their corner for them.'

Harry frowned and steepled his fingers on the desk before pausing to say, 'But don't you see? You could do a lot of good as by constant checks on the ventilation and particular pit practices, you could be responsible for preventing accidents and even deaths? Tom Langstone has been doing the job for years, in your opinion is he fit to continue?'

Tobias squeezed his cap between his hands and shook his head. 'No, everyone knows he's too old now. He's a proud one though, is Tom. In any case, I'd be robbing him of his job if I accepted it. He's got a family to feed.'

Harry smiled. 'We'd find something else for him up top, something less dangerous. Granted, he'd get less money but there would be benefits like easier work for him and don't forget, my father left him some paintings in his will, they'd be worth a bob or two.'

Tobias nodded. 'Let me think about it.'

'Look, before accepting,' said James. 'Have a

word with the men if you like after we've called Tom in to tell him we have a new position for him. Obviously, don't discuss it in front of him.'

Tobias's eyes flashed dangerously. 'Just what do you take me for, Mr Wilkinson? Of course, I'd never do that. If the men want me to take over his job though if Tom's happy to take on the new role whatever that may be, then that will be a different kettle of fish.'

'Very well,' said Harry. 'We'll give you time to think about it.'

Tobias nodded at both men, then replaced his flat cap on his head and left the office, closing the door behind him.

'What do you think?' James exchanged glances with Harry.

'If the men agree, I think he'll have half a mind to go for it.'

And so by the end of the day, Tom was put to work above ground upon his agreement and Tobias accepted the role of foreman. None of the men had objected to this as most thought Tom was too old to do the job and had been for a long time —safety was now paramount for the bosses at the pit. The men had a lot of respect for Tobias and welcomed him as their new foreman.

***

With a skip in his step as Tobias left the pit, he made his way towards Rose Cottage to see Cassie, he couldn't wait to tell her the news about his promotion. Secretly, he was pleased to accept the post but didn't want to be boastful in front of the other colliers. Cassie would be home this afternoon as she was only working a half-day she'd informed him. Fleetingly, he thought back to what Harry had said to him about not mixing pit business with home business but he figured on this occasion the man wouldn't mind him sharing his good news with her. All thoughts of Rose waiting for him later at the tea room were pushed from his mind.

***

As Cassie gazed out of the cottage window she noticed Tobias walking up the path, immediately her mind was drawn back to the day of the attack by Anthony Fairley. She swallowed hard and then patted her hair down before opening the front door of the property to greet him. She wondered what he wanted. He had cleaned himself up a little since leaving the pit, at least, he'd washed the coal dust from his face and hands but his clothing was still coal-blackened. In his hand, he held his metal snap tin that was common for miners to use to keep their food in underground as it kept out the damp and most importantly of all, any rodents that might come sniffing around.

He beamed as he approached the doorstep. 'Good afternoon, Cassie!'

She noticed now since that awful incident he'd dropped the "Mrs Hewitt" approach.

'Good afternoon, Tobias,' she greeted. 'What brings you here today?' She realised that her husband had given him a bit of a ticking off since his last visit to the cottage but how could she possibly turn him away after he'd come to her rescue like that the other day? She wondered if he'd turned up to keep an eye on her maybe to ensure Fairley hadn't returned.

He cleared his throat and then his smile widened, it was obvious to her that he was puffed up with pride, maybe it was because he'd seen that newspaper article about himself. 'I've just been promoted!' He announced.

'That's wonderful news! You'd better come inside and tell me all about it. The boys are upstairs sleeping.'

He nodded tentatively as if unsure. 'I...I don't know if I should step a foot inside after what Mr Hewitt said the last time I was here.'

She nodded. 'I can understand that but I think it will be all right on this occasion as long as you don't make too much a habit of it. In any case, I'll be seeing you soon at the schoolroom after hours when I'll be introducing you to some great works of fiction and non-fiction from my husband's book store.'

He nodded gratefully. He'd almost forgotten about her promise to do that. Often, he found that people promised all manner of things but failed to deliver though it was evident Cassie wasn't one of those sorts.

'Come on inside,' she coaxed. 'I'll put the kettle on to boil.'

He nodded and smiled as he removed his flat cap from his head, wiped his feet on the doormat and stepped over the threshold of the property.

Within minutes they were seated at the kitchen table as he told her all about his surprise promotion.

'It's no surprise to me,' said Cassie as she poured tea into his awaiting teacup. 'I could see from that first time when I was sitting in our coach at the pit that you had something about you the way you commanded those men.'

Tobias grinned and then nodded sombrely this time. 'Things can get out of hand for the bosses like if the men get out of control with their thinking.' She offered him a plate containing a slice of fruit loaf that was slathered generously with salted butter, gratefully he took the plate and began to devour the cake, closing his eyes as he did so. He opened them to find Cassie watching him with a smile on her face.

'I love watching you eat,' she said. 'Now then what is the actual position you'll be taking?'

He laid down the half-eaten slice of cake back on the plate. 'It'll be as an underground foreman. I'll be responsible for ensuring there's plenty of ventilation in various areas, checking on the amount of coal hewn that day, that sort of thing. I'll need to keep records an' all. To be honest that's what's bothering me most.'

'But why on earth would that bother you? You can read and write, you told me so.'

'Oh, aye. I can do all of that but my handwriting's not the best. It's kind of scruffy like as I didn't have all that much schooling. I'd love to write in joined-up writing like the toffs do.'

'Well, that's no problem. I can also give you some writing exercises when we meet and teach you how to write in joined-up handwriting too. Also, I know how to keep books as I have to do them for the tea room.'

He let out a long breath and the look of relief on his face was evident to Cassie.

'You're so good to me,' he smiled. 'That's a weight off my mind. Now about you, how are you feeling today after your ordeal the other day?'

Heat infused Cassie's face and she fought to say the words. 'I...I've found since that I can't sleep properly. Harry, Mr Hewitt, has noticed as he's found me asleep downstairs most mornings. I really don't know what to do about it.'

Tobias looked at her with great empathy in his ebony eyes. 'That's understandable, you had a great shock that the man could approach you like that behind your husband's back. I doubt though he'll try it again as he knows I know. As long as I'm around, he'll not lay another finger on you and will stay away.'

She nodded but all the while thought: *What if one day you are no longer around though, Tobias?*

As if he could read her thoughts he smiled. 'Don't worry, I plan on staying around a long while yet.'

She relaxed and lifted her teacup to take a sip, almost absently as her mind wandered as she tried to quash all thoughts of that man and what he had tried to do to her. Finally, she laid down her teacup on its saucer and said, 'So, with more responsibility will come more money for you?'

He nodded. 'That is one of the benefits, yes. Now, listen to me before you change the subject. My mother is good with herbs and things, she can sort you out with a little potion to help you sleep at night. She makes it from boiled nettles and one or two other things. Works wonders.'

'Oh, I don't know whether I should...'

'It won't harm you none. I've tried it myself when I was having problems sleeping a while ago after that explosion. Thoughts of Mr Hewitt Senior and young Benny Brewster dying that day kept running through my mind. I kept thinking, why them and not me? So Ma made me up a concoction to take at night. Didn't taste all that good I'm warning you in advance like, but it did the trick.'

Cassie relaxed and then smiled at him. 'Then I shall try some. Thank you so much, Tobias.'

A thought occurred to Cassie as Tobias had mentioned Harry's father there. She paused for a moment before asking, 'How did you find working under William Hewitt?'

He shrugged. 'He was fair enough to us workers I suppose and respected an' all but I do think he turned a blind eye to the kids working underground. Some of them should'na been there, they were underage.'

She nodded. It all seemed to tie in with what her husband had told her. William Hewitt had lived two separate lives: one honourable and one that in her book, lacked integrity.

They were both chatting away so amicably that Cassie hadn't noticed the time nor the fact that her husband's coach was drawing up outside the cottage until she heard the sound of the coach door being slammed shut. Harry was home.

Chapter Ten

As Clyde entered The Furniture Emporium he glanced across at the tea room to see Rose inside serving an elderly man and woman with a tray of tea and an assortment of cakes. She looked up when she noticed him passing by and smiled. For the first time since she'd told him she was stepping out with Tobias Beckett, he felt like smiling back at her and he did so and gave a little cheery wave as he used to do before it all happened but he didn't pause to make silly faces at her through the window as he would once have done nor did he step inside for a chat. He just went about his business of loading furniture onto the back of the cart with his brother.

'Glad to see you're finally over that "Rose Business",' Jem said with a smile.

Clyde nodded. 'T...there's no use in b...being bitter, is there?'

'None at all.' Jem slapped him on his back. 'Good man, Clyde. You've grown up a lot lately.'

Clyde realised his brother wasn't just referring to how he reacted towards Rose now but because he'd stopped spending money like water and knocking around with nefarious sorts. When his brother entered the emporium and he waited outside for him to return on the horse and cart, Clyde thought there was something a little different about Rose today but he couldn't quite think what it was. Her hairstyle was just the same, swept up in a neat chignon knot so that it didn't fall across her face when she was serving customers. Polly hated it if she found a single hair in any of the food, she thought it best not to give any of them the chance to complain. Rose had told him that once. No, it wasn't Rose's hair that was different, it was her dress. Of course, she was wearing her Sunday best one with the pretty blue flowers on it. That's what it was that made her look different. Usually, she wore a dark dress beneath her white frilled pinafore to serve customers. But why was she so dressed up today? Thinking no more of it as now Jem had returned and was taking charge of the horse's reins, he dismissed it from his mind. It was now none of his business anyhow as she had a new beau.

'Never mind, Clyde,' Jem said sympathetically as the horse took them in the direction of Drisdale to deliver some furniture, today they were dropping off an oakwood bureau and a sedan chair for the Horton family, 'there'll come a time when Rose won't be on your mind anymore, lad.'

Clyde figured his brother was right but that wouldn't happen any time soon as far as he was concerned, he'd always hold a candle for Rose Barton.

***

Cassie froze mid-sentence when she noticed her husband walking up the path. She exchanged glances with Tobias who did not look in the slightest bit perturbed by the man's arrival. The front door clicked open, there were some muffled sounds as Harry removed his coat and hat as he hung them on the hall stand and slotted his cane in the holder, then the kitchen door opened wide.

'I'm home!' He shouted and then his eyes fell upon Tobias who was still seated at the table halfway through his second cup of tea. But to Cassie's surprise, her husband did not look angry at all. 'Hello, young man,' he greeted. 'Came to tell my wife the good news, I suppose?'

'I did, yes.' He swigged the dregs from his cup and standing said, 'Well, I'll be off. I don't want to disturb your evening.'

'That's not a problem at all. We won't be eating for another hour or so. I finished business earlier today. Would you like a glass of brandy with me in the living room?'

Nervously, Cassie held her breath, hoping Tobias would decline but instead, he accepted. Her heart sank as the longer he remained in their home, the guiltier she would feel about the secret they were keeping from Harry.

Harry approached her and kissed her softly on the cheek and the pair excused themselves to go into the living room while Cassie went to attend to the boys upstairs. By the time she'd fed and changed them, Harry and Tobias were sitting like a pair of bookends on either side of the fireplace, chatting away amicably, drinking brandy from their best crystal glasses. Harry did not appear to care either that Tobias was in his working clothes. This was a turn up for the books, all of a sudden, Tobias seemed to have gone up in the world at Marshfield Coal Pit and held in great esteem by her husband.

It was a further hour before Tobias said his goodbyes and both men sounded a little worse for wear as they had knocked back the brandy so quickly. 'Call here any time!' Harry shouted after Tobias as he closed the door behind him and then returned to the living room.

'You've changed your tune?' Cassie arched a curious brow in her husband's direction.

'Yes, I have. I misjudged the man as I viewed him as a troublemaker but now, I think he's an asset to have and of course, he's now been promoted.'

Cassie smiled genuinely pleased about that but she had to admit she was relieved when Tobias had finally left their home. She felt all right when she was alone with him, but when Harry was around she felt as though she was doing something sinful. It was wrong of course to keep what happened the other day a secret but she would eventually tell Harry but in her own time.

***

As Tobias made his way merrily home, reflecting on what a good day it had been, he noticed the tea room light was still on and then he remembered Rose's offer. It appeared as if the last customer was leaving and Rose caught his eye and beckoned him over with a wave of her hand. What could he do? He'd rather resist temptation and head off straight home to tell his mother and his siblings the good news but maybe now he could tell Rose too.

He drew the tea room door open and marched over to where she stood and said, 'I was promoted at work today, Rose! You are now looking at the new underground foreman!'

Rose's eyes lit up like a pair of beacons. 'Oh, Tobias, I am made up for you.' She kissed his cheek and glancing around to ensure no one was watching them, she drew him to her and wrapped her arms around his neck, not at all worried about dirtying her new dress on his coal-dusted clothing.

He inhaled her sweet perfume and planted a kiss on her lips. Oh, it felt good to have her body next to his but he really should go home. Lifting his hand she placed it over her breast and he felt himself harden with desire for her.

'Come on inside the tea room,' she whispered. 'I'll lock the door.'

Eagerly, he followed after her and watched as she turned the key in the lock and drew all the curtains. A lantern was lit on the counter which gave a subtle glow as she took his hand and drew it up inside the skirts of her dress, placing it on her thigh. He groaned. 'Are you sure you want this?'

'Yes,' she murmured. 'Nevermore so...'

Pushing her back against one of the tables, he said, 'Lie across there.' Then he was on top of her doing all the things he'd longed to be doing for such a long time but now it wasn't Rose beneath him feeling his touch, it was Cassie. His tongue plunged into her mouth and he tasted her sweet lips. Then he was dragging her drawers down and experiencing her wetness for him as he was about to enter her as she gasped.

'Slowly, please...'

That brought him to his senses as he realised she was untouched by any man and now it wasn't Cassie anymore it was Rose beneath him, quivering to be taken gently. But he was past the point of no return and he could be gentle with her, he could take his time and she did want him after all. It wasn't as though he was forcing her and his head was swimming from the brandy as he entered slowly. All the while he was checking she was all right and she was replying that she was as she let out some gasps and he guessed that he had broken her maidenhood and there was no going back now, so rhythmically he bucked his hips slowly at first and then with slightly more force so that they were as one and after a time, he was surprised that she was enjoying it too. Then as that moment came when he gave up his release, it wasn't Cassie he was thinking of anymore but his own sweet Rose.

**

Several minutes had passed before reality sank in for Tobias as he stood there staring at her sprawled out in a most undignified manner across the table. What had he done? He'd now despoiled Rose, who until she'd met him had remained a maiden. He looked at her aghast as she straightened up her clothing and smiled unsurely at him.

'Are you all right?' he asked her. But this time he wasn't asking in case he'd physically hurt her now he was more concerned about her well-being. Did she regret what had just occurred?

'I think so.' Rose dismounted the table and retrieved her drawers which she found on the floor near an adjacent table. She pulled them on over her boots and sliding them up her legs, once safely in place, she then allowed her dishevelled dress to drop down over them. 'Please don't worry,' she said, brushing the creases out of her dress. Then taking him by the arm, she added, 'This was surely meant to be.'

Tobias frowned. 'How do you mean?'

'You've got that promotion now so that will set you up and I've got my job here so we can make plans for our future together.'

Oh, he did like her and all. She was a beautiful young woman but at the moment he didn't want anyone or anything to tether him to a post, and especially not for life. He opened his arms towards her and she went to him and then he held her for the longest time as he inhaled her sweet perfume. 'When you go home, have a good wash,' he advised. 'You know just in case.'

Even in the dim light cast by the lantern on the counter he could see her frowning. 'I can't do that when everyone is in the house,' she pouted. 'My Pa would wonder what's going on as I only bathed in the tin bath and washed my hair last night when my brothers were at the pub.'

'Look,' he said sombrely, 'what we did there might cause you to fall pregnant if it's your time of the month when you can conceive.'

She nodded and then bit her lip. She did look beautiful and all as now her hair was dishevelled and it had found its way out of that chignon knot and lay in waves on her shoulders. She deserved someone so much better than him, why hadn't she stuck with Clyde? It was obvious how he felt about her but women were strange creatures like that often going for the men who treated them badly. Oh, he wasn't a bad man himself, far from it, he did a lot of good for people but he was a free spirit and didn't plan on being shackled in chains for the rest of his life. 'I suppose I can manage a wash down below in a tin bowl out in the privy when I get home,' she murmured with her head down, then she looked up at him, 'but I wouldn't mind having your baby inside of me, Tobias.'

He lifted her chin with his thumb and forefinger. 'Please don't ever say that, I'm simply not worth it. You deserve someone better than me.'

'No, I don't!' She began to sob as reality now hit home for her too. He was telling her that he was going to move on from this as it had just been a momentary lapse on his part. It was now clear to her that he didn't picture her as part of his future but saw some other man beside her instead.

'Please don't cry, Rose,' he soothed as he softly caressed her cheek. 'Now straighten yourself up and pin your hair up and I'll walk you safely home. We can remain friends though, can't we?'

She nodded through sobs but it was obvious she was distraught. Maybe he did have a kind of love for her in a protective sort of way but the flame he had for Rose was a small one in comparison with the huge inferno he felt for Cassandra.

***

Over the following few days, Tobias avoided passing the tea room when he could and other times when he had to, he kept his head down and didn't stare across or wave as he once had. Fortunately for him when he went to the pit first thing in the mornings, the tea room was closed, it was in the afternoons he needed to be most careful. Hopefully, the girl would get over him given time, and although he had enjoyed making love to her it was all part and parcel of his celebration for getting promoted that day that had sparked it all off. If he hadn't been knocking back the brandies with Harry for a couple of hours, then he would have kept his head and not called into the tea room at Rose's request, he'd have walked right on by.

His new job at the pit gave him extra responsibility and was more of a challenge for him but he was the sort of person who thrived off a challenge. The main thing was the men trusted him and some would even say they entrusted him with their very lives.

***

'I don't know what's the matter with the girl!' Polly was moaning about Rose to Cassie one afternoon when she'd called to the cottage to see her. They were both seated at the kitchen table. It was a hot day, heavy and humid and looking at the clouds outside, Cassie thought they might be in for a thunderstorm.

Handing Polly a glass of cool homemade lemonade she sat down opposite her and poured one for herself. 'How do you mean?' she frowned.

Polly shook her head. 'She's not herself lately.'

'But you told me she's in love?' Cassie took a sip from her glass and set it down on the table.

'Ah, but that's it you see,' said Polly tapping the side of her nose with her index finger. 'I think something's gone wrong there.'

Cassie's heart thudded heavily. 'How'd you mean?'

'She no longer mentions that Tobias one and the other day she came into work with her eyes all swollen and puffed up as if she had been crying over something so I reckon it's all over between them.'

Cassie nodded. 'She is young though and now Tobias has a lot of new responsibility at the pit.'

Polly angled her head to one side. 'Yer always defending Tobias. I've noticed that. You like him a lot don't you?'

Cassie laughed nervously. 'I suppose I do, he's been good to me, put it that way.'

Polly narrowed her gaze, it was obvious she was going to keep on until she discovered exactly why Cassie thought so highly of the young man. She was like a dog with a bone who was nibbling off the last bits of meat, gnawing and gnawing away until she got what she was after.

Cassie sighed. 'I don't think he's perfect, not by a long chalk,' she found herself saying quite candidly. 'It's just the fact he fights his corner and particularly those of others that I admire so much.'

Polly sniffed loudly and then she crossed her hands one over the other and pursed her lips prudishly. 'Yes, that was evident enough from that front-page newspaper article I read. It's not that though that makes me wary of the young man.'

'Then what is it, Polly?' Cassie looked at the woman curiously. Polly was never one to keep things inside. What you saw was what you got with her.

'It's the fact he has some sort of hold over Rose. She's been mesmerised by the fellow ever since they first met, and if you ask me, it ain't healthy! And now he's gone and upset her for some reason. She won't speak to me about it, would you have a try? She likes you. To her, I'm just the boss who's on her back all day long, but well...you have a way with folk that I ain't got.'

Cassie smiled. 'I will speak with Rose if you want me to, but I don't want to interfere between the pair of them as I've started giving Tobias reading and writing lessons, he's doing very well too.' She frowned. The last thing she needed was a load of grief right now as she had her own problems to attend to.

'Really?' Polly quirked a curious brow. 'Seems to me you have enough on your plate as it is, my girl!'

Cassie forced a smile. 'It's no hardship. Sometimes he calls to the cottage on his way home from work and other times he'll call around to the school for half an hour when I'm due to lock up. He's a quick learner and all. He's not a beginner, he can read and write but wanted to learn to write longhand. I've just been suggesting various books he might like to read which Harry has loaned him from the book shop, and I've been showing him how to write in longhand. He's almost mastered it already. But I will have a word with Rose as you suggest, but I'm not getting involved in anything by coming between them. I shan't mention this to Tobias, mind you.'

Polly smiled. 'That'll do me then, Cass. Can't have no waitress at the tea room with a face as long as a horse.'

'I tend to agree with you there, Pol. It's not good for business.'

'Speaking of the tea room, are you likely to return any time soon?'

Cassie paused and exhaling said, 'Not for the foreseeable future. I spoke to Mr Newton, the headteacher, just this morning and he'd like me to remain. He reckons I'm an asset to the school. In fact...' She wondered what Polly would make of this, 'he asked me would I consider training to become a teacher as the boys and girls have taken to me and I can command a classroom as well as any of his staff!'

'What do you know!' Polly enthused. 'I always knew you had it in you, girl!'

'How do you mean?'

'Ever since you first arrived at Marshfield Manor I thought you had something about you. You're intelligent and you ask questions.'

Cassie raised her brows. 'So, you think I should train to be a school teacher?'

'Yes, I think you should, it would be quite fulfilling for you. Oh, I know you've enjoyed running the tea room in the past but it's not enough for you these days as it's no longer a challenge. You need new horizons, a new dream to plan for.'

As Cassie gazed out of the cottage window and down onto the picturesque village below, she realised Polly was right.

***

The following morning when Cassie had a break from the school she made her way to the tea room to speak with Rose. Polly was right about the long face. The girl looked like she'd lost some weight too and her usual sparkling eyes were dull and seemed larger than usual. Cassie put her hand on Rose's shoulder and led her to a quiet table in the corner as Doris brought them a pot of coffee. When they'd both seated themselves and Cassie had poured the coffee, she looked into Rose's eyes. 'Now what's the matter, Rose? I've been told you're not yourself at the moment.'

Rose sniffed and then extracted a handkerchief from her pinny pocket, she dabbed at her brimming eyes. It was a moment before she could find the words to say. 'I'm sorry, Mrs Hewitt. You are right, I haven't been myself lately as I've done a very silly thing which you'll think badly of me for when I tell you. I ain't told a soul apart from Doris about it.'

'Doris must be a trustworthy friend as she hasn't mentioned a word to either myself or Polly.'

Rose smiled. 'I'm glad of that, I knew she'd be loyal to me.'

'Yes, she's a good sort is Doris. So, what happened?' She asked lowering her voice.

Rose blew her nose on her handkerchief and took a sip of her coffee before setting her cup down in its saucer. 'The evening that Tobias got promoted...'

Cassie felt her heart sink. This was all about him and she wondered what he might have done that was so bad for the girl to be in this sort of state.

'Yes?'

'I'd asked him to call to the tea room after I finished work. I would be the only one here and had the key to lock up,' she hesitated before quickly adding, 'I didn't know then about the promotion or even if he'd show at all. But he did and it was evident he was over the moon about being promoted. I smelt the brandy on his breath and realised he'd had a few drinks but I didn't mind as he seemed nicer somehow.'

'Nicer?' Cassie arched a brow.

'Yes, more interested in me if you like. Anyhow, he called inside the tea room and one thing led to another,' she lowered her voice surreptitiously and glanced around herself before adding, 'and then it just sort of happened, Mrs Hewitt.'

Cassie's blood ran cold as it finally dawned on her what exactly had happened. 'So you mean you had relations with one another here in the tea room?'

'Yes,' Rose said in barely a whisper as she lowered her head as if in shame. Then she looked up at Cassie with a tinge of regret reflected in her eyes.

'And you're sorry for what happened?'

'Oh yes, Mrs Hewitt.'

'And Tobias?'

'He was happy at the time but soon went cold on me afterwards. He walked me safely home but not without letting me know first that he didn't plan on sticking around any longer!' She raised her chin as if in defiance. Deep down, Cassie realised the girl's despair was now turning to anger at being rebuffed in such a fashion.

'That's dreadful.' Cassie sighed. She'd seen it happen before, many a young girl had fallen for someone who no longer wanted to hang around once he'd got what he wanted from her.

'It wasn't really his fault. I didn't realise he thought so little of me...' she shook her head sadly.

'Well, hopefully,' Cassie stretched her hand across the table to pat Rose's, 'no real harm will have been done. If I were you I'd not say anything about this to anyone else not to sully your reputation.'

Rose chewed on her bottom lip. 'I think it might be too late for that, Mrs Hewitt.'

Cassie shook her head. 'Oh no!' She said as her hands flew to her face as she pre-empted what Rose was going to say next and she hoped upon hope that she was wrong. 'You mean?'

Rose nodded. 'I think I'm pregnant, my courses haven't arrived this month.'

Cassie squeezed the girl's hand. Tobias had definitely gone down in her estimation. One moment he'd been a knight in shining armour at The Grange School as he'd rescued her from Anthony Fairley's clutches but now he was a scoundrel, a rotter in Cassie's book for the way he'd treated poor Rose.

***

When Cassie had returned to the school and

Polly was out of earshot, Doris stared hard at Rose. 'What did Mrs Hewitt want you for?'

Rose felt her face grow hot. 'Nothing,' she mumbled.

Doris's eyes flashed. 'Don't give me that Rose Barton, she was here with you long enough and appeared to be most secretive. I couldn't even hear what the pair of you were saying, you were whispering so much!'

Rose shook her head as her eyes filled with tears. 'All right,' she sniffed as she watched Polly turn her back at the counter to boil up the tea urn. 'Remember I told you I did it with Tobias?'

Doris slowly nodded her head. 'How can I ever forget?' Then suddenly she blurted, 'I 'aven't told a soul, on me honour.'

Rose smiled through her tears. 'I know you haven't, but Mrs Hewitt wanted to know why I wasn't myself so I told her the truth.'

Doris put her hand over her mouth before dropping it. 'Oh, my goodness. Will that get Tobias into trouble now as he works at the pit for her husband?'

'I don't know and I no longer care. He left me high and dry!' Rose said haughtily as she stuck her chin in the air.

Doris narrowed her eyes. 'Folk will find out soon enough and who will support you and the baby then?'

'I'll manage. I have my job here.'

'But you'll have to finish here when you're near

the birth and find someone to look after him or her. I reckon you at least ought to get Tobias to cough up some of his wages every week.'

'I don't want another thing from that man!' Rose spat out the words angrily.

'If that's the case and so far only you, me and Mrs Hewitt know who the father is, then I would quickly find yourself another father for the child.'

Rose gasped at what Doris was saying to her. 'You mean have relations with someone else so they think they're the father?'

'Yes,' said Doris in a conspiratorial tone of voice. 'Find someone decent and let them believe the child is theirs. You can always pretend the infant has arrived prematurely.'

Rose rubbed her chin. It was a thought for sure that might be the answer to her dilemma.

'It could get yer out of a sticky situation,' Doris said mischievously. 'If yer 'aven't burned all yer bridges with Clyde, I'd start seeing him again as you did really like him when yer were seeing him.'

Rose nodded as her mind raced ahead at an alarming pace. She could start by waving at Clyde as he passed by and offering him a free custard slice and a cup of tea when she was alone in the tea room. The more she thought about it, the more she liked the idea. But she'd have to catch Mrs Hewitt and tell her she was mistaken about the pregnancy and inform the woman that her courses had finally arrived late instead of not at all.

Chapter Eleven

Clyde was walking past the tea room window when he heard a knocking sound. He glanced in that direction and saw it was Rose frantically waving at him from the window. That was odd, at this time of an evening the shop was usually shut. He nervously lifted a hand to return the wave after glancing across the street in case she was waving at someone else and not him. That would have made him feel like a great big buffoon, but he was cheered to discover it was definitely him she was waving at. When he arrived at the entrance for the stairs up to the emporium, Rose had already left through the side door of the tea room and was waiting for him.

'H...hello, Rose!' he smiled at her. 'What are you doing here so late?'

'I was just about to close up when I wondered if you'd like a cup of tea and there's a leftover sticky bun.' She smiled almost shyly at him.

Clyde had to admit that he was ravenous, he hadn't eaten since midday. His eyes lit up as he nodded eagerly. 'T...thank you,' he said with some excitement. Within a minute or so he found himself seated at one of the tables while Rose fussed around boiling up the tea urn. Then she took a tray containing two cups, a teapot and the bun over to the table.

She watched silently as he munched away on the bun before saying, 'I am sorry about what happened between you and me.'

He nodded. 'You're happy with Tobias though, aren't y...you?'

She shook her head and then dabbed at her eyes with a handkerchief. 'No,' she sniffed. 'I broke things off with him just last night.'

Clyde's eyes widened. 'But w...why?'

'Because he's not you, Clyde. I realised quite early on that I'd made a mistake and should have stayed with you, but pride got the better of me. I listened too much to what folk had to say about people who had money. I thought it might change you but I can see it hasn't at all. Will you forgive me?' She stretched across the table and patted his hand.

He nodded, hardly believing his ears. His sweet Rose was telling him she'd made an error of judgement and now he was wondering if she wanted to return to him. 'Y...yes of course I forgive you.' He smiled at her still smitten. 'W...would you like it if things returned to how they were when we were stepping out with one another before Tobias came along and your father seemed annoyed by my inheritance?'

'Oh, yes please!' She smiled broadly as she relaxed back into the chair. The first part of her plan had gone smoothly. Doris was right, it wouldn't harm for folk to think he'd fathered her child. Now all she had to do was to lure him into making love to her. It wouldn't happen tonight, maybe she'd have to be persuasive and coax him gently as she was sure that Clyde wasn't exactly a man of the world and she was sure she was his very first girlfriend.

And so, it was arranged that she and Clyde were now sweethearts once again with Rose ensuring that she visited Cassie at the cottage the following day to say she'd been mistaken as her courses had arrived late and what a relief that was! Thankfully, the woman had informed her that she hadn't mentioned the "so-called pregnancy" to anyone, not even to Polly and as far as Polly was concerned, Rose was nursing a broken heart

***

Tobias was underground having a word with Abraham Mason who had his twelve-year-old son, Alfie, working beside him. Alfie had been helping his father for the past few months to carry the tools for him and fill the drams with lumps of coal after his father had cut or blasted them. He was a good lad who had just started as a pupil at The Grange School.

'How's it going, Alfie?' Tobias asked as he turned towards the lad and held up his lamp so he could get a better view of him.

'I'm all right, Mr Beckett.' he said, lowering his head as he answered.

Tobias had noticed the men and boys now referred to him in a more formal manner than when he'd been simply one of them and was then known as just "Tobias". 'We're not overworking you, are we?' Tobias chuckled. He liked Alfie a lot as the lad was a hard worker and keen to please.

Abraham draped a kindly arm around his son's shoulders. 'No, he's keeping pace very well.'

Tobias waited for Alfie to reply but he just nodded. Something wasn't right and he felt like Abraham Mason might be pushing his son to get the work done, but then he noticed something else as Alfie began to walk away towards the awaiting dram, he dragged his right foot, pausing every so often, before continuing.

'What's the matter with the lad, he's limping badly there?' Tobias frowned.

Abraham let out a long groan and then he sniffed as if about to cry. 'It's no good, I'm going to have to tell you the truth. My son caught his foot underneath a dram wheel yesterday, he wasn't quick enough to get out of the way.'

Tobias had seen some crush injuries at the pit in his time so it was natural for him to be concerned. 'And what has the doctor said about it?'

'That's just it,' said Abraham with a sound of anguish in his voice. 'The doctor hasn't examined him.'

'Why ever not, man?' Tobias's hackles rose with anger.

'B...because I can't afford it. My wife, Ginny,

cleaned Alfie's foot and strapped it up last night but we couldn't afford no doctor not with eight mouths to feed at home and another on the way...'

Tobias felt a sudden surge of sympathy for Abraham. It wasn't that the man didn't want his son to receive medical attention, he simply couldn't afford it. 'I'll tell you what,' said Tobias, 'I'll ask Mr Hewitt or Mr Wilkinson if we can send him to the doctor and if they'll pay for it.'

'That's never happened before here,' said Abraham. 'They've always made the workers' pay for their own accidents. Mr Wilkinson's father was too mean to shell out.'

'Well,' Tobias patted the man's shoulder, 'that is set to change while I'm here. I'll see if I can find one of the bosses to ask. Meanwhile, rest the leg until I return and if anyone accuses your lad of shirking, tell them he's in urgent need of medical attention and I've gone for help.'

Abraham nodded. 'I'm so pleased you've got this job, Mr Beckett. Old Tom would have just left him working in that condition.'

'Hopefully, we'll have caught it in time before any further damage is done,' Tobias said sagely and he made his way up to the surface to see one of the bosses.

Thankfully, Harry Hewitt agreed that the lad needed attention and he sent both Alfie and Tobias in his coach to see Doctor Medway in Marshfield. He was reputed as charging fair prices and had a good reputation.

As Tobias sat in the doctor's surgery which was housed in a large wing in the man's house, he did his best to reassure Alfie though he could tell the lad was in some discomfort as he winced and groaned from time to time. As they waited, he noticed Rose Barton, leave the doctor's consulting room, scurrying off with her head down, almost as though she didn't want anyone to notice her presence. What on earth was she doing here? Surely her surgery would be in Wakeford? He was about to leave Alfie's side to speak with her as he feared something was amiss when he noticed her friend, Doris, rise from a chair to escort her out of the building. He hadn't noticed Doris when they'd first seated themselves. It all went out of his head though when it was Alfie's turn to see the doctor. A nurse in a navy dress, long white apron and starched hat, stood beside Doctor Medway as he enquired kindly about what brought Alfie here today. It was obvious he was from the pit due to their coal-dusted clothing and Tobias thought the doctor probably had a fair idea they were here due to some mishap at Marshfield Coal Pit.

Doctor Medway ordered the lad to lie on the consulting bed. Tobias lifted Alfie and settled him down on the bed, then a nurse rolled up the lad's trouser leg and removed his thick woollen sock and homemade dressing, she winced as she did so.

'And what have we here?' Doctor Medway's face showed concern, but then he suddenly smiled at the lad. 'I can see you have some sort of injury, how did you manage that?'

'It were the wheels of the dram, me foot almost got trapped under one of them,' Alfie said in barely a whisper so that the doctor had to strain to hear him.

'I bet that hurt like the Devil?' Doctor Medway raised his brow. 'But don't worry, I think it's something I can sort out for you.'

'Yes, Doctor,' Alfie said now speaking in a normal tone of voice, obviously feeling reassured by the doctor's manner. 'I felt like screaming but didn't, not to frighten me Pa.'

'Now,' said the doctor as he examined the foot and leg, 'I'm going to press in several places and you just tell me where and when it hurts, all right?'

Alfie nodded.

Tobias watched the doctor thoroughly examine the leg and foot and then asked the nurse to roll up the other trouser leg and remove that sock too. 'I'm just comparing and contrasting both limbs,' he explained to the nurse who nodded at him.

'Yes,' he said finally. 'It's as I suspected, a small fracture I think and a little inflammation of the area too which I can give you some ointment for, but you'll need to keep it clean while it heals. Count yourself lucky that you got your foot out in time as a crush injury can be very severe indeed—you've had a very lucky escape by the seem of it. So I think it best you keep away from the pit for a good six weeks and rest that leg. No other treatment will be necessary as I think it's only a small bone in the foot that's broken, the foot has a lot of those.'

'Thank you, Doctor,' Tobias said, relieved it wasn't something more serious but he guessed the management and the lad's father wouldn't be very happy to know he would be away from work for a few weeks. Neither could afford such a loss.

They took the coach back to Alfie's small house on Flannagan Street, where his mother was waiting frantically on the doorstep while a couple of neighbours fussed around her. 'I just received the news that he'd been taken to the doctor, thank goodness,' she cried. 'I wasn't happy about him going to the pit this morning. I wanted him to stay in bed and send one of his brothers for the doctor but we couldn't afford it.'

Tobias alighted from the vehicle as the woman approached and he smiled at her. 'I've just accompanied your boy to the doctor's surgery in Marshfield, Mrs Mason, so he has received medical attention. He was attended to by Doctor Medway who gave him a very thorough examination. Don't worry, Alfie's quite all right, he's been a very brave lad. Apart from some pain and bruising, the doctor thinks he may have broken a small bone or two in his foot which will heal up on their own as long as he stays off work for the next few weeks and rests his leg. He's also given me an ointment for you to apply to the wound in case it becomes infected. The nurse dressed it up with bandages and she's given me a couple of spare to give to you along with a few dressings.'

'What a relief!' said Mrs Mason, placing the palm of her hand to her chest as she let out a long breath.

Tobias touched her lightly on the shoulder and smiled as the woman's eyes brimmed with tears as her two neighbours chatted amongst themselves. 'Now then, if you will open all the doors for me to carry him inside the house. Where can I settle him down?'

'On the old couch near the fireplace will be best as he'll be warmest there and his father can carry him up the stairs to bed tonight.'

Tobias nodded and then returned to the coach to tell Alfie the plan. The lad was now beaming broadly, probably relieved his foot injury would be all right and the fact he'd get a few weeks' break from work being attended to and fussed around by his mother had probably put that smile on his face.

He lifted Alfie down from the coach as the boy wrapped his arms around his neck and now more neighbours had popped out to see what the fuss was and why there was a posh coach parked in their street. It was more common to see costermonger carts here than coaches or carriages.

Once settled down on the couch, Alfie's mother covered him up with a warm woollen blanket and placed a pillow beneath his head.

'I'll leave you to it then,' said Tobias handing over the bandages, dressings, and the tin of ointment. 'Remember the dressing is to be checked every day and the ointment to be applied twice a day until it runs out. Doctor Medway was clear

And what about their widows and their families when they died? It all makes me bloody sick!' He spat out the words as if they were venomous and maybe to him, they were.

James's face reddened at the mention of his father. He whispered something to Harry who nodded.

'Very well,' said Harry. 'What we'll do is discuss this with the co-operative with both Anthony Fairley and Mr Middleton to see if we can all come to some sort of arrangement, at least for the young lads if they suffer an industrial accident.'

'Good luck with that!' said Tobias turning his back on both men as he marched out of the office and slammed the door hard behind himself.

***

'That didn't go as expected,' said James as he exchanged a subdued glance with Harry.

'No, it didn't, but the man has a point, we have a duty to those men and boys and we did say we wanted things to change around here. It's all or nothing as far as I'm concerned. Sadly though, we've inherited a legacy from our fathers where we are left to pay for their sins.'

'Never was a truer word spoken. I'll try to have a word with Fairley today and perhaps you could approach Mr Middleton?' He arched an eyebrow in Harry's direction.

'Yes, but I'll need some courage for that.'

'No problem. I'll pour us both a strong brandy before we leave here.'

Harry chuckled, feeling he was going to need it after the morning he'd had. First discovering the boy was injured, then the rush to get him emergency help, backed into a corner by Beckett into paying for the medical aid and now maybe having to dip into the colliery coffers to pay for the lad to lie on a couch for the next six weeks! He accepted the glass of amber fluid from James's outstretched hand, took a sip and felt it warm the very core of his being.

He didn't realise taking this place on, along with a business partner, would have so many ups and downs. It seemed there was more friction going on outside the pit involving social-economic issues than inside it when the men were working. That young lad Alfie though must have had a lucky escape with that dram, it must have just nipped his foot as he pulled it out of the way as otherwise, it might have been a crush issue which could possibly have left him lame for life or without a foot at all. They needed to learn lessons from this.

Chapter Twelve

The Headmaster of The Grange School advised Cassie that around thirty years ago the government had created a programme for teacher training. It allowed both men and women to enter into the teaching profession but these days trainees would also have to attend a pupil-teacher centre, the nearest of which was at Hocklea. Government grants were issued for the teaching programme and this allowed middle-class women to become involved in the classroom.

Cassie figured she had nothing to lose by enrolling on this programme and so the very next day she set out for Hocklea where she needed to obtain the necessary paperwork. She had a character reference from Mr Newton in her reticule at his suggestion, just in case, they required one before giving her the forms.

After leaving the education office with the necessary paperwork, she was deep in her thoughts thinking what a surprise this would be for Harry if she were accepted when she noticed a familiar couple of figures walking in front of her. Clyde and Rose! But what were they up to? Surely Clyde hadn't taken the girl back after she'd left him for another like that? The way though he was holding tightly onto her hand and she was practically snuggling into his chest, she guessed he had.

She trailed them along the street until they stopped outside a jewellery store. It wasn't any old jewellery store either, this was *Fletcher's Finest Jewellery*, which was held in esteem and had undoubtedly set the highest prices far and wide in these parts. It was one of those stores the wealthy loved so much as they received first-class attention from Mr Fletcher and his plum-in-the-mouth staff. The furnishings inside the store were those that you'd see at a fine manor house and indeed, she and the lord had once been customers themselves. Though Cassie hadn't realised when Oliver was lavishing her with expensive gifts that their funds were fast flying out of the window, else she'd never have accepted the silver and gold jewellery he'd bestowed upon her encrusted with emeralds, diamonds and pearls. All were seized and sold off to cover his debts after his death.

Clyde was pointing out something in the window and Rose was nodding her head, gazing up at him and smiling, and then they both disappeared inside the shop. What on earth was going on here? She had a bad feeling about this. But what could she do? It was none of her business whatsoever except that Rose was her employee at the tea room, even if she wasn't there to supervise at the moment, Polly was in her place. She'd ask the woman if she knew anything about it when she returned home later.

***

'I'm sorry,' Harry said as they were both seated at the dinner table. 'I don't think teacher training is the right thing for you to do right now.'

Cassandra's lower lip quivered. 'But why ever not? You've always supported me in the past?'

'I know I have and will continue to do so but first let me explain. Tobias has whipped the men up again about being paid for any accidents that occur, so that their medical bills are paid off and that they received some sort of pay whilst off sick.'

'That's only right, isn't it?' She frowned and bit her lower lip.

'Yes, it is of course. But we need to sort all that out, find some way of paying for it. I don't like to ask you this, but would you consider the profit you make from the tea room as an investment into this scheme?'

Cassie's mouth dried quite suddenly and she found the words hard to form as though they were somehow stuck on her tongue, until finally, she said, 'That would be a risk. I've built that shop up from scratch and have three employees. It doesn't rake in an enormous amount of money but enough to give us a reasonable living, whereas you seem to take little from that coal pit!' As she raised her voice, she surprised herself with the venomous tone of it.

Harry smiled sheepishly. 'I do understand all

that of course I do, my sweet. But it would help us through a tricky situation as we're trying to reform the pit and all that goes with it.'

Cassie huffed out a breath of annoyance. Then she tossed her cotton napkin on the table and stood to leave but first, she pressed her knuckles into the table with such force that they were white, before saying, 'No, no, no! I will have no part of this! My tea room is nothing to do with your bloody coal pit!'

Harry looked up at her with sad eyes. 'Tell that to the likes of Mr and Mrs Mason while their son is off work for six weeks and there are eight mouths to be fed...' he said slowly shaking his head.

'What about James Wilkinson? He's now living in what was my house and I've heard his wife, who sits on her backside all day long except for the times she entertains and shows her face at charity events, is spending his wealth right, left and centre to show off what she has to her cronies. Ask her to stop spending and contribute half and then I might think about contributing something from the tea room profits!' Without looking at her husband, she fled from the table and quickly made her way upstairs, throwing herself on their bed as she buried her face into the pillow and wept. Her dream for a better future was fast becoming a nightmare for her.

***

James Wilkinson had not got very far with Anthony Fairley regarding the proposed co-operative idea to pay young workers when they were off sick or injured from work. He was facing Harry when they'd both gone for a drink in The Swan Hotel in Hocklea, they were seated either side of the fireplace on a settle, each with a low copper-topped table between them.

'So, the man couldn't be persuaded then?' Harry raised a brow in his direction.

'No, there was no budging him at all. He reckoned such a scheme would be wide open to all kinds of abuses.'

'He might have a point there I suppose.' Harry scratched his chin and stared into the flames of the fire almost as though that's where the answer lay, but of course, it was in his own mind.

'Probably, but I think he's just too mean to put the welfare of his workers before profit at the mill. If it wasn't for your good lady wife speaking to him, I doubt he'd have agreed to The Grange School opening in the first place. He's always held her in high regard.'

'You're probably right,' Harry smiled and then shrugged his shoulders. He lifted his silver tankard and took a long slug of ale from it before settling it back down on the table. This was proving to be a trying day for him, if something wasn't sorted out and soon, he just knew he'd have Tobias rallying him on behalf of the colliers. This wasn't going to go away.

'What else can we do? You've spoken to Mr Middleton?'

'Yes, he's quite an affable chap and said he'd be prepared to consider our suggestion.'

'At least he's on our side. I say, I've just had another idea!'

Harry frowned as he knew what James and his ideas were like sometimes. 'Go on then, what is it?'

'Why don't we send Cassandra around there on her own to charm the man?'

Harry laughed nervously. Then he shook his head vehemently. 'That would be like pimping my wife out. I don't like it at all. It's already caused a rift between us that I've asked her to invest some of her profit from the tea room as it is.'

'Aw, these women and the big ideas they get. It's just a little hobby to her though, isn't it? Something to keep her occupied?'

'No, it is not!' Harry's eyes flashed. 'The tea room means more to Cassandra than that. She set it up against the odds when the rest of the villagers were against her and to tell you the truth, I'm bloody proud of her!' He gritted his teeth and clenched his fists as if ready to go a few rounds with James who raised his vertical palms as if in defence.

'I'm sorry. I can see I've hit a nerve there. I'm just so used to Adeline mooching around the house all day long and having various cronies calling in to see her for afternoon teas. She's not hard-working like your wife is and to be honest, hasn't got the same level of intelligence. She'd far rather splash out on the latest fashionable gowns shipped over here from Paris, or decorate the rooms with expensive wallpaper and paint, not to mention all the new furniture we seem to have acquired of late. Her charitable work gives her some sort of prestige I suppose, but that's only a face showing exercise—she feels the need to be doing good so her name gets mentioned around fashionable society. She'd never roll her sleeves up and offer any practical help. Oh no, she's been carried around on a satin cushion for far too long!'

Harry nodded. 'Then it's high time you took her in hand and curtailed her spending sprees, my fine fellow!'

James glanced at his partner as though the man had just showered him with ice-cold water. He narrowed his eyes before widening them once again. 'I say, do you really think I should curtail her expensive habits?'

'Yes, I do,' said Harry sagely. 'We've a pit to run between us and if that carries on the way it's going, we'll all end up in deep water. I suggest you get her to speak with a financial advisor who can let her know exactly what she's spending and give her a monthly allowance which, if she goes over, she then has to do without!'

James nodded silently with his mouth wide open. This wasn't going to be simple for him, Harry had no doubt. The only trouble was that it might not be as easy as they first thought to convince Adeline that's her spending should be cut. It would be easier said than done.

They ordered another round of drinks before leaving the hotel to board their awaiting coach. On the journey back to the pit, Harry stared out of the window. In the distance, he could see mountains, trees, fields and the odd cottage peppered against the mountainside and all the time he wondered how James's wife could be such a cold-hearted, frivolous person when there was so much need in the area. It warmed his heart to think of how kind Cassandra was, she could melt the coldest heart and it gave him an idea.

***

Rose smiled at the shiny sapphire and diamond ring on the fourth finger of her left hand. 'Oh, it's simply gorgeous!' She enthused as Clyde stood beside her in the jewellery store.

'Shall I pack it up in the velvet box for you, miss?' The assistant asked. He was a man who appeared to be around seventy-years-old to Rose and she wondered if he was Mr Fletcher himself but then as she glanced up at a painting of a distinguished-looking gentleman in a top hat sat astride a sleek looking horse, she guessed that was Mr Fletcher, not the assistant. She exchanged glances with Clyde, who nodded.

'I think it best we put the ring away for n...now,' he said firmly. 'We have to make an o...official announcement and first, I need to ask your father for your hand in marriage.'

She smiled at him. 'Yes, but I think you and I can consider ourselves engaged, Clyde, even if no one else knows?' She gazed at him in expectation as he nodded eagerly. Her main objective was to get him to perform the deed and now she felt if they were engaged he would be far more likely to do so out of wedlock. In a sense, she felt sorry for him as he was rushing into this engagement without much thought other than it might make her stay with him. There was one thing, it had taught her a valuable lesson and she was prepared to stick with him for life now. One day they'd have more children, so Clyde could also have his own offspring but as far as she was concerned, providing Doris managed to keep her trap shut, no one need ever know. She thought she'd done a good job of persuading Cassie she'd made a mistake about the pregnancy. In any case, when the time came for her to give birth she could go and stay with her grandmother in Hocklea and return a few weeks later. No one need know exactly when the baby would be born and she was quite sure that Clyde wouldn't be counting the months, and even if he did, she could easily convince him the baby was premature. But what about her father? What would he say when Clyde asked him for her hand in marriage? She dreaded to think. And Jem too? She'd seen the looks he'd been giving her ever since she'd taken up with Tobias Beckett. It wasn't going to be easy by a long chalk.

Chapter Thirteen

Cassie was strolling around the marketplace with her wicker basket over the crook of her arm early one morning when she bumped into Tobias out of the blue. 'Hello, Cassie!' He beamed at her.

She was genuinely pleased to see him, though a little wary now after hearing how he'd recently acquired intimate knowledge of Rose's body. Hesitating for a moment, she cleared her throat. 'Good morning, Tobias,' she said stiffly, noticing he was smartly-dressed this morning in what appeared to be a new tweed jacket, white shirt and brown bow tie, his trousers had a sharp crease down the front, his shoes were well-shined and he even had a bowler hat on. He looked more like a toff than someone who worked underground at a coal pit. It was evident he'd gone up in the world lately.

Before she had a chance to ask where he was going, he explained. 'I'd better tell you what I have planned, I'm off to have a word with Anthony Fairley as he's refusing to take part in the co-operative's suggestion of paying young workers when they're off sick or injured from work. He's more interested in the profit he makes than what his young mill workers endure.'

'Oh!' she said feeling quite surprised. 'But why have you been asked to see him?'

'I haven't. Your husband and Mr Wilkinson don't know about this. I think after what he did to you he owes us a favour which I am about to reclaim.'

Cassie's mouth dried up. She opened her mouth to say something and closed it again. 'I don't know if you ought to do that,' she said tentatively. 'It's bad enough my husband wants the profits of the tea room to be ploughed into the pit and he's put me off training to be a teacher, but now I feel like both of you are prostituting me for your own ends!' Tears filled her eyes as they misted over and to her horror, her legs began to buckle beneath her. She hadn't long since taken Emily to the church school and she'd felt fine then. Before she hit the floor, two strong arms helped her onto her feet. Taking her basket from her hand and placing a reassuring arm around her, Tobias ushered her away from the busy marketplace through the throng of people. 'Come on,' he said softly, 'Mr Fairley can wait. I only live over there. I did promise to get my mother to make up a potion to help you to sleep, it's there waiting on the shelf in the pantry for you. She'd be only too happy to brew you up a cup of tea.'

Cassie smiled weakly at him. Why did he have to be so handsome? That dark unruly hair, those ebony eyes, that wicked smile. She could see what Rose had found so appealing about him, but to her, he spelt one word, *danger!*

***

Rose had shown up on Doris's doorstep soon afterwards to show the girl her engagement ring, but she didn't want folk on the street seeing that dazzler on her finger as who knew who might be watching and not only could news of her impending engagement get back to her father before she'd had time to gently land the news on him or Clyde was to ask for her hand in marriage, but maybe someone might try to steal the ring from her finger. People were pretty poor around these parts. So, she ensured she wore her gloves to conceal it.

Doris blinked before asking, 'What did yer want to see me about? Is it something to do with the tea room?'

'No,' said Rose as she bubbled up with so much excitement that she felt fit to burst. 'Is there somewhere we can speak in private?'

'Aye, you can come through to the scullery if you don't mind going in there, that way we'll not be disturbed.'

Rose nodded amicably and followed her friend through the narrow passageway and out to the scullery. Rose guessed the family were in the living room.

Doris drew out a chair noisily across the flagstone floor from the old pine table and gently said, 'Take the weight off yer feet for a bit.'

Rose smiled and then grimaced as she massaged

her back before sitting down. 'Thanks. My back plays up now and again these days.'

Doris pulled out the chair opposite and seated herself. 'Now what was it you wanted to see me about?'

'This!' said Rose as she removed her gloves to show her left hand across the table to the girl.

Doris's eyes enlarged. 'You mean you're...'

'Engaged? Yes.'

'But when did this all happen?'

'Just yesterday. That was why I took the afternoon off. Clyde took me into Hocklea to purchase the ring from Fletcher's.'

'Fletcher's!' Doris let out a low whistle and, fortunately, her parents were in the next room, else they'd have boxed her ears for whistling like that. They didn't hold with girls doing that sort of thing but she just couldn't help herself. 'And it's a sapphire then?' Doris's eyes grew large.

'Yes, sapphire surrounded by miniature diamonds. Oh, Doris, I've never owned anything so lovely in all my life!' Her eyes lit up as she spoke. 'But when I leave here I'll hide it beneath my glove, then I'll put it away in its box in a safe place under my bedroom floorboard when I return home. I have the task of telling Pa soon and I don't think he'll be best pleased, so I don't want anyone else to see it before then. Clyde has offered to go to see him to ask for my hand in marriage, but I don't know about that...'

'Rose,' Doris began. 'I'm pleased for you and

Clyde, honestly, I am.' She chewed her bottom lip. 'But I think you need for Clyde to approach your father as he will be going about things in the correct fashion that way. Then if your father refuses you can think again, but I don't think he will. The sooner Clyde does it the more it will look as if it is Clyde's baby you're having.'

In all the excitement, Rose hadn't considered that. 'You're right, Doris. The sooner Clyde goes to see my father the better. Are you really pleased for me?'

'Yes, of course, I am.'

Rose placed her index finger to her lips. 'Not a word to anyone for now though until it's official? Jem needs to be told and all and I don't know how he's going to take it.'

Doris nodded. 'You have my word,' she said smiling. 'Now how about a glass of ginger beer to celebrate?' Both girls giggled.

***

Tobias led Cassie by the arm towards Market Street, which was a short distance from the open marketplace. The houses here were small and appeared crammed together, beside them was a long alleyway running between that street and the adjacent Bridge Street. 'Nearly here now,' he coaxed as Cassie found putting one foot in front of the other made her feel as though she were wading through a mountain of jelly as she clung on to his arm.

Finally, they arrived at a house that had a very

clean looking doorstep and he pushed open the door to lead her inside. 'Ma!' he called out, which caused a little woman with white hair, dressed in a long dark dress and flowered pinafore to come scurrying towards them.

'What's happened? You only just left here a few minutes ago?' Her bright, beady eyes were darting all over the place, then they fell on the state Cassie was in and she helped lead her inside the property. 'Sit down by the fire in the armchair, dear,' she said looking at Cassie with concern. Then turning towards her son as Cassie took a seat, she whispered. 'What on earth has happened?'

Tobias led his mother towards the small scullery. Not wishing to tell her the full story, he just said, 'She came over faint after having a little shock.' Though of course, he didn't tell his mother that he was the cause of it as he was prepared to front up Anthony Fairley and demand that he engage with the co-operative else he'd tell Harry about what had occurred at The Grange School.

His mother nodded. 'But who is she?'

'She's Harry Hewitt's wife, Ma. The one you've made that sleeping potion for.'

'I see. I'll give it to her later. I'll go and brew up. The poor lady looks like she's in dire need of a sweet cup of tea.'

Tobias nodded. His mother was a good 'un. A salt of the earth sort who would do anything for anyone, any time. In fact, people often knocked on their door to ask for a potion for this or that. His mother wasn't a witch or anything like that, more of a herbalist who could sense sometimes what was wrong with folk and what they needed to take. Whether it was nettle tea to settle the nerves or a soothing balm for a skin complaint. Some people trusted her more than the doctor.

'Are you all right now, Cassie?' Tobias asked taking the opposite armchair by the fire.

She'd been staring at her hands on her lap. She was wearing only one glove. 'It's my glove, I think I've lost it,' she murmured vacantly.

He nodded. 'It must have happened when you almost fainted.'

'Y...yes. I remember removing it as I was about to fumble in my basket so I could pay one of the stallholders, it must have happened then.'

'I'll just run across and see if I can find it for you.' Tobias shot her a smile.

Noticing how nervous Cassie was when Tobias dashed off, Tobias's mother appeared at her side with a cup of tea. Smiling at her, Cassie accepted. 'Thank you, Mrs Beckett.'

'You drink that up, gal,' the woman reassured. 'Where's Tobias shot off to now?'

'I dropped my glove in the market when I almost fainted there,' said Cassie.

'I've never known that one so gallant!' Mrs Beckett chuckled, then she took the armchair opposite Cassie. 'My son tells me you've had some difficulty sleeping of late?' She raised an inquiring brow.

'Y...yes.' Cassie gazed down into her cup and lifting the spoon from the saucer, slowly stirred it as if by doing that it would give her something to focus her mind on. She could hardly tell the woman that the cause of her lack of sleep was something Anthony Fairley had done to her. Even Harry didn't know of that. Setting her spoon back down on its saucer, she met the woman's eyes. 'Something traumatic happened to me and I've had trouble sleeping ever since.'

'Now don't you go worrying,' Mrs Beckett said. 'I've made that potion up for you from nettles and feverfew. Try some of that at bedtime in some warm milk and you'll soon drift off.' She fumbled in her pinafore pocket for a moment to retrieve a small brown bottle with a cork stopper which she handed to Cassie.

'Oh, thank you, Mrs Beckett!' Cassie placed the bottle in her basket. 'How much do I owe you?'

'Nothing at all. I often make up potions for folk.'

Feeling overwhelmed by the woman's generosity, Cassie's eyes brimmed with tears, then Mrs Beckett tapped her hand. 'Seems like that trauma you went through caused you a right upset. I'll tell you what...' she said kindly. 'When you've finished that cup of tea, I'll read your tea leaves for you. How about that?'

'Oh, I don't know.' No one had ever read her tea leaves before or told her fortune in any sort of way. She bit her lip as suddenly Tobias burst in through the door.

'I've found your glove!' He shot her a disarming smile as he handed it to her.

'But where was it?'

'One of the stall holder's found it and kept it safe for you.'

'Want a brew, son?' His mother asked.

He nodded eagerly but not before his eyes widened. 'What's going on here? I feel like you pair are up to something?'

Mrs Beckett nodded. 'I just offered to read Cassie's tea leaves for her.'

Cassie squirmed in her seat. 'Oh, I don't know about all that stuff.'

'Let her do it,' Tobias said gently, then when his mother had departed to fetch his tea, he whispered, 'She enjoys it enough and has a real gift you know.'

Cassandra smiled weakly at him and nodded. 'Very well.' Although she wasn't all that interested in discovering her fortune if it amused Mrs Beckett to do so, she'd comply. It was the least she could do to repay her kindness.

'I think I'll leave you both to it for now,' Tobias winked at her.

Cassandra raised a vertical palm. 'You're not still going to see Mr Fairley, are you?'

'No, not if it's going to upset you. I might whip up some public opinion in The Ploughman's Arms instead and get the lads together to protest outside the mill instead.'

Cassie frowned. She didn't much like the sound

'Yes, he is.'

Mrs Beckett shook her head. 'I don't think it's him though.' Then quite suddenly, her eyes clouded over and she said, 'Sorry to cut it short, I can see no more.'

Baffled by how quickly the woman shut the prophecy down, Cassie let out a slow breath. Maybe it was just as well not to be able to see into the future anyhow. She thanked the woman for the tea and the potion too, offering to pay for it again, but Mrs Beckett just smiled and shook her head.

'Honestly, it is a pleasure for me to do these things. I've been in good health for most of my life and to see others benefit from my knowledge, makes me so happy.'

Cassie left the small house with a promise that she'd call again at some time in the future when she was passing by.

Chapter Fourteen

Tobias faced Anthony Fairley in the man's office. 'Please take a seat,' the man proffered his hand in the direction of a vacant chair opposite the desk in which he sat. It was obvious by the disconcerted look in his eyes that he'd been caught off guard when Tobias had shown up without warning.

Tobias cleared his throat. 'I'll stand if it's all the same to you. I'll just say what I've come to say and then I'll be off.'

Mr Fairley extracted a silk handkerchief from the inside pocket of his jacket to mop the perspiration from his brow and replacing it said, 'Oh, yes? And what might that be?'

Tobias pursed his lips, anger now coursing around his body which he needed to keep in check, if he were caught even verbally abusing the man, never mind thumping him, he'd be thrown off the premises, so he needed to tread carefully. He took in a deep composing breath and let it out again. 'It's like this you see, Mr Fairley. I have certain information on you that you wouldn't like getting out. Wouldn't like it at all as it would discredit you in front of your wife, your family, your peers within the general community, not to mention of course one Harry Hewitt!'

Fairley's face flushed and he swallowed hard. 'Go on,' he urged.

'Now it's about that co-operative thing to allow the young lads and lasses some payment if they are sick or injured from work.'

Fairley shook his head. 'I thought you might say that,' he said as he inserted a couple of fingers beneath the collar of his shirt as though it were too tight for him all of a sudden. Then as if trying to compose himself, he steepled his fingers on his desk and forced a smile.

'You thought right then, didn't you? All I ask is that you give your agreement to the co-operative that you're on board with the idea of paying your young workforce money for their keep while they're ill or injured by machinery or whatever. Their families can't afford to lose another wage earner in most cases...'

'And if I don't agree?' asked Fairley, his eyes widening.

'If that is the case, then it will cost you far more,' said Tobias. 'It will cost you your reputation in this area.'

Then before he was forced to take a swipe at the man, he left his office realising he had given him plenty to think about. As he marched out of the place, he heard the echoing noises of the metallic clanks and whirring from the machinery as a frenzy of activity took place. It was a soulless place where the Devil himself presided in that office above looking down on his workforce. And if that Beelzebub of a boss wasn't prepared to shell out for his young staff, then Tobias was prepared to take things further to tarnish the man's reputation with a big brush of sticky, smelly tar!

But Tobias needn't have worried as the very next day back at the pit, he was called into the office by Harry Hewitt and informed that Anthony Fairley had decided to comply with the co-operative's request after all, and it was evident the way both Harry and James Wilkinson were eyeing him up curiously that they wondered if he had a hand in it. Tobias had raised his vertical palms at the time and chuckled. 'Not I! But aye, it's a good thing the man's finally relented!' He'd said. How could he possibly explain that he'd forced the man's hand by threatening blackmail over the nasty incident with Harry's wife? Questions would be asked of him so he decided it best to act all innocent about the issue. Whether both bosses believed him or not, mattered not a jot, as long as the children were taken care of that's all that counted in the end.

***

The twins were growing into such big boys and Cassie took delight in them. It was now autumn and the leaves were falling from the trees in a cluster of such beautiful colours, she'd never known an autumn like it. Russet reds, burnished gold, ambient ambers, all trodden crisp underfoot. James Wilkinson had presented her and Harry with a double baby carriage so they could take the twins out walking to the park or down to the village. It was an absolute Godsend. Cassie had slowly cut down her hours at The Grange School now that all the staff was settled in. She'd decided if she couldn't train to be a teacher then she might as well return to the tea room. Polly was more than happy with her return and when Cassie was there in charge, she often took care of the boys for her, but today they were both in attendance at the tea room as Edna was taking care of her grandsons and Emily was at school. The little girl was coming on leaps and bounds and her teachers often extolled her virtue, explaining that she was even ahead of some of the older children at the school when it came to reading and writing. This made Cassie so proud. She realised she should be happy with her lot in life having a hardworking husband and such beautiful children, as well as a business that she'd set up herself. But something was missing. She hadn't been aware of it until Tobias Beckett had come into her life and turned it upside down.

'So, you mean to tell me,' said Polly as she put the tea urn on to boil, 'that Mrs Beckett indicated you might be going on a journey on a ship?'

Cassie nodded, chewing on her bottom lip. 'She said one or two other things as well, but when she got to the part about a dark-headed man entering my life she suddenly cut short the fortune-telling!'

Polly raised a brow. 'Happen she meant your Harry as he's dark?'

'I thought that too, but no, it wasn't him she said.'

Polly's eyes grew large. 'I'm wondering if she meant her own offspring, Tobias!' The woman blurted out suddenly.

'Good heavens! I hope not!' Gasped Cassie. 'Surely not?'

'It might be him though, why else would she cut it short like that when you reckoned you had to be talked into it in the first place?'

Cassie nodded. She could see what Polly meant, though she hoped there was some other reason for it. Changing the subject, she said, 'I notice Rose and Clyde seem to have got close again lately.'

'Oh, yes,' gleamed Polly. 'I think we might be seeing a wedding on the horizon there!'

Cassie gasped. In a way, she hoped not, in her book it was far too soon for that. She'd seen them both looking in the jeweller's window of course but now she wondered if they'd been looking at rings.

'What's the matter?' Demanded Polly. 'Yer've gone as white as a sheet?'

'A couple of weeks ago, I saw them both looking in a jeweller's window. It wasn't any old jewellery store either, it was that posh one in Hocklea.'

'So?' sniffed Polly. 'Naught wrong with that is there?'

'I suppose not. It's just I don't want to see Clyde hurt again. She hurt him badly the last time.'

'Perhaps he's grown a thick skin since then,' said

Polly hopefully.

'I'm not so sure.' Cassie stared at Rose as she and Doris served a few customers on two tables that were joined together as if they were some sort of party. They'd just taken a large order for that table. Rose was setting down two fancy tiered cake stands as Doris placed two large china teapots on the table beside those.

Polly nudged her with her elbow. 'Yer worry far too much, Cassie. That's always been a failing of yours. Yer'll see, things always have a way of working themselves out!'

Cassie hoped that on this occasion, Polly was proved right.

***

Clyde couldn't believe his luck, not only had Mr Barton invited him inside his home that evening but he'd seemed positively pleased and shaken his hand uproariously when he'd asked for Rose's hand in marriage. It had all gone like a dream.

'I don't like the sound of it,' Jem had said later. 'It was well known that the man didn't want her to marry you. I reckon something is up. Maybe that Tobias Beckett dumped her or something and her father's happy that you're the first fool to fall for her charms since. I reckon he must have deflowered her or something!'

Clyde felt his bubble burst. 'Do not say things like that, Jem!' He shouted at his brother. 'Rose isn't like that. She's a maiden and we plan to have children. I'll n...not s...stand by and hear her name tossed to the wind like that!' Clyde held his chin upright and glared at his brother. He felt like punching him on the nose right now. He hadn't felt that way in a long time, not since Jem had threatened to sell Rose Cottage and move out of the area.

Jem held up his vertical palms. 'All right, lad. I'm sorry. Maybe the gossip I've heard is wrong. I just got the impression she was soiled goods, that's all. But maybe you're right and maybe someone or another want people to think that way about her. It's your happiness I care about. I don't want to see you hurt again, that's all.'

Clyde nodded, realising that his brother had his best interests at heart. 'I d...don't want us to fall out, Jem. Just never let me hear you call her over again.'

'I promise,' said Jem, nodding. 'You'll not hear anything bad about Rose from me ever again but what I can't promise you is that others won't say anything bad about her.'

'If they do, they'll have to reckon with me,' said Clyde fiercely and it was in that moment Jem came to a realisation.

'You're really in love with Rose, aren't you, Clyde?'

'Yes, I am,' Clyde said through brimming eyes. 'I'd die for her, Jem.' Then he began to cry as his brother held him in his arms.

***

The men back at Marshfield Pit were slapping

Tobias on his back and shaking his hand. 'I don't know how you did it,' said Abraham Mason as he pumped Tobias's hand, 'but I'd like to thank you. Now my Alfie can safely rest up without being totally docked for it.' He stopped shaking Tobias's hand and stepped back to say something of a serious nature to him. 'I know the lad won't get full pay but from my understanding from Mr Hewitt and Mr Wilkinson, he and the other lads here will get half pay. At least it will keep the wolf from the door for a while and it's a load off my mind, let me tell you. I were that worried how we'd cope with my missus having another baby on the way!'

The men were all stood beside the pit entrance with the enormous pit wheel towering above them like a mighty giant, a large pile of coal was banked up in front of it and the tall, red chimney stack puffed out smoke as they waited. The pit office and other outbuildings were in the distance behind them. To the right of those was the railway line which transported coal in trucks to neighbouring villages like Hocklea and Drisdale. The men were well-rested as they were about to begin an afternoon shift.

Tobias smiled. 'Yes,' he nodded. 'It won't be just at this here pit either but at the cotton and wool mills an' all. Those lads and lasses need fear no more. If I had my way I'd get full pay for them as you know. Most of these accidents and illnesses that occur are work-related anyhow, so the least the bosses can do is to cough up, I reckon. My brothers and sisters work at both mills and so far, they've been paid by their own money if they've ever taken ill or had an accident. Thankfully, nothing serious has occurred as yet, just minor things, but it might happen and what then? Those kids can't speak up for themselves, so I'm their mouthpiece if you like.'

'How'd you mean?' Abraham frowned.

'There was a sick fund established and money kept back. A penny taken from their pay each time. So, it's their own money they're bloody getting back! Now what should be happening is that they don't have to pay at all as most of their illnesses and accidents are caused by the mills anyhow, they're industrial diseases and accidents. Did you know there's a kind of cancer you can get from the oil in the mule spinning machines? Apparently, if you lean against it too long every day, you can get cancer of the groin and even of the mouth from the kissing shuttle from sucking the cotton thread through the shuttle.'

Abraham shook his head. 'Thank goodness we all have you on our side fighting for us, Mr Beckett!' Then he turned to the other men. 'Three cheers for our comrade here!'

Three cheers went up loudly and Tobias felt his face redden. He hadn't asked for any praise, indeed he would have been happy if no one had realised he'd had a hand in this. He hoped Abraham Mason wouldn't ask any questions of how he'd achieved a very good outcome, but he needn't have worried as the man patted his forearm before leaving to attend to his work, and winking at him said, 'You've got the gift of the gab for sure, Tobias.'

Tobias followed the men inside the pit, happy enough for time being.

***

Following what had turned out to be a long shift, Tobias made his way home across the mountain and he passed the tea room. It was dark now and there was no light on inside much to his relief. He thought it odd that Rose no longer badgered him. How could she go so cold all of a sudden when she'd been as hot as a flame for him at one time? Still, it suited him at the moment for her to stay away from him. Harry Hewitt's book store was all in darkness too but the centre stairwell between both shops was lit and glancing up, he could see lights on in the furniture emporium on the floor above. Almost as though it was destined to be, Clyde emerged through the front door that led to the emporium closely followed by Jem. The lights had now gone out, they must be packing up for the night he thought.

Noticing him in the shadows, Jem called "Goodnight!" across the road to him. Tobias was about to reply when Clyde began marching over to him and began pushing him in the chest with the heel of his hand. 'Stay. Away. From. Rose Barton!' He threatened.

'What's going on here? I haven't been anywhere near her recently, Clyde.'

'It had better stay that way. She's marrying me now. She's my girl and we're engaged.'

Tobias could hardly say he didn't want her now as that wasn't strictly true, he did like her, he just hadn't liked the intensity of the relationship and that was why he'd cooled off. 'Sorry, fella,' he said amicably. 'You won't be getting any bother from me.'

'Come away!' Yelled Jem at his brother. 'Leave Tobias alone. You heard him, he's not having anything to do with Rose no more.'

Clyde made a loud grunting sound and as if thinking better of it, he turned his back on Tobias and headed for the cart. What had got into Clyde though, he was normally so mild-mannered? This was most unusual for him. Rose had given him the impression when she took up with him that she and Clyde were just friends. Oh well, it was none of his business now—that ship had sailed a long time since.

'Sorry about that!' Jem shouted at him and Tobias just nodded, dug his hands deep in his pockets and carried on walking back home.

Chapter Fifteen

Cassie and Emily were together, she realised she hadn't been able to give the little girl much attention lately as the boys and her work at the tea room took up a lot of her time. So today, after school instead of Edna picking Emily up, Cassie did as a surprise for her.

'Mama!' Emily shouted as she bounded out of the classroom and into her mother's open arms.

Cassie held her daughter tightly to her chest and planted a kiss on the top of her head. 'Have you had a good day, poppet?' She asked.

Emily looked up at her with big wide eyes. 'Yes, Mama. Miss Adams says I'm the best in the whole class now at reading and writing. She says that I'm the most intelligent little girl she has ever known!'

Cassie chuckled. 'Did she now?' She wondered if perhaps her daughter was exaggerating or Miss Adams told all her pupils they were the best at something or another.

Noticing her mother's levity, Emily frowned then folded her arms as her lips formed a pout. 'No, Mama! It's all true! Miss Adams told me she wants to have a word with you about me.'

'Very well, dear.' Cassie took her daughter's

hand. 'I shall make time to see her but now I'm taking you out for your tea today.'

Emily looked up at her mother. 'At the tea room?'

'No, not at the tea room, you go there quite enough. There's a little place that's opened up that serves hot pies. I thought we could have one of those with some mushy peas, if you like?'

'And lashings of gravy too, Mama?'

'Yes, lashings of gravy too!' Cassie smiled.

'How are you picking me up today though, Mama? Where's Grandma Edna?'

'She's taking care of Gil and Ernie for me so I can spend some precious time with you, my beautiful girl.'

Emily beamed. She'd not had her mother all to herself for some time as the boys always hankered after Cassie's attention.

As they turned the corner on Mulberry Way, Cassie paused. For a moment it felt as though she were robbed of all breath. *Tobias!*

'Hello, both!' he greeted. He was smartly-dressed again this afternoon as though he'd been attending to some business.

'Hello,' Cassie said nervously. 'What brings you in this direction?'

He shot her a disarming smile. 'I have a confession to make, I noticed you headed here and wondered what you were up to but I can see you are in some lovely company.' He patted Emily's head and she smiled at him. 'And what's your name, young lady?'

'Emily.' She shyly put her chin on her chest.

Tobias's gaze fell back on Cassie. 'So, where are you both headed?'

'To that new pie shop around the corner.'

'Thought you'd check out the competition, did you?' He chuckled.

Cassie smiled. 'No, that wasn't my intention really, it was to spend some time with my daughter.'

Tobias's eyes widened as though maybe he should leave them both be. 'I'm sorry, I don't wish to intrude on your precious time together.'

'It's no bother,' said Cassie.

Then suddenly Emily said, 'You can come with us if you like?'

'Oh, I wouldn't wish to impose...' Tobias said shaking his head.

Cassie noticed the disappointment on her daughter's face and said, 'It would be no problem at all. Emily wishes you to come with us.' She looked at him with expectation.

He nodded, then crouching beside the little girl so that they were of the same height he said, 'Emily, I would love to accompany you and your mother to the pie shop.'

Emily beamed and then she ran ahead skipping all the way.

'That was very nice of you to do that for her,' said Cassie.

'It's my pleasure,' he said as they walked beside

one another. Tobias caught her eye as she felt a little flutter in the pit of her stomach.

What on earth is happening to me? Every time I'm in this man's company I am becoming more of a nervous wreck inside.

Because he excites you! Came the answer from her inner voice.

While they found a table at the steamy pie shop, Emily went to pat the owner's sheepdog who was sleeping beneath one of the tables. For a moment, Cassie startled, afraid the dog might hurt Emily even though she had a dog of her own, who at the moment had remained at Hawthorn Cottage with Polly and Aunt Bertha.

'It's all right,' Tobias soothed across the table. 'The owner's dog is called "Pip" and he's soppy with children. He's well-used to people.'

Cassie nodded and let out a long breath. 'Thank goodness for that. I don't want to come over as being one of those overprotective sorts of mothers but I do worry as Emily sees the good in everyone and everything. In fact, she can be a little too trusting at times.'

He studied her face for a moment. 'You could almost be describing yourself there, Cassie,' he said without smiling and she realised he was right about that.

'What makes you say so?'

'Oh, the way you welcomed me into your home that afternoon I turned up without warning when you were home with the twins asleep upstairs.

It was obvious your husband didn't want me invading his home nor speaking to you there.'

She smiled nervously. 'I suppose that is the truth but he doesn't seem to mind so much nowadays.'

'He's changed his opinion about me, but you...' he stretched out and patted her hand across the table, sending a shock wave coursing around her body, 'you trusted me from the very onset. Why was that?'

She drew in a long breath and let it out again, her face was feeling a little hot and she hoped her cheeks weren't flushed with embarrassment. For a few seconds, she watched her daughter patting the black and white dog beneath the table which was a few feet away, as she tried to formulate the words to say. 'I think it was that time when I first laid eyes on you from our coach when you were speaking to the men at the pit. You seemed so sure of yourself and spoke with such passion and conviction, and,' she paused for a moment, 'it was obvious that you had the backing of the other colliers. I realised then that you were someone who could be trusted.'

He smiled for the first time, unsurely, 'I didn't realise you'd seen all that?' he said. 'I mean I noticed your husband's coach there that afternoon, but I had no idea anyone else was watching.'

It was obvious he was taken aback and it was his turn to be at a loss for words. He caught her eyes, his own dark and shiny as he said, 'I realised the first time I ever met you, Cassie, that you are a kindred spirit. You have that passion in you too but it's hidden.'

She nodded. 'I do indeed.'

'What is it you really want to do in life?'

She swallowed hard for a moment. 'I want to train to become a teacher. I've loved every moment of helping at the school but I've watched those teachers and feel I could do the same.'

'What's stopping you then?'

She shook her head and to her horror, her eyes began to mist with unshed tears and that lump in her throat had returned. 'It's my husband. I told him of my dream, and usually, he's so supportive of what I want to do, but he thinks it's enough for me to work at the tea room and look after the children, cook and clean, and generally just keep house. It's a man's world all right.'

Tobias nodded slowly. 'I know what you mean. It doesn't fulfil you. I've often thought of leaving this country...' He said in barely a whisper.

'Leaving? But to go where?'

'America. I've heard they're crying out for men with my coal mining skills in places like Pennsylvania and Ohio. An Emigration agent is coming to Hocklea next week. He'll be speaking at the town hall there and taking names of those interested parties.'

For a moment, Cassie felt bereft. If Tobias left, he'd take that spark of passion she shared with him away for good. She opened her mouth to say something and closed it again. Then finally, she said, 'But you must do whatever you think is best for you.'

'If you emigrated too, you could train as a teacher in America,' he said his eyes flashing.

Her stomach fluttered again. 'But Harry would never want to leave here. He wouldn't leave his mother anyhow nor his business interests.'

'Then come with me,' Tobias said suddenly.

'*But the children!*' This was absurd, she could never leave her life behind, but hadn't she done that when the Lord had passed away?

'We could take them with us. Oh, Cassie, I know deep down inside you feel the same way I do. I've seen that yearning in your eyes. You married your husband thinking you'd live happily ever after and maybe you do love him...'

She nodded. 'I do.'

'But it's not enough for you. *He's* not enough for you. You yearn for excitement, a little danger in your life. Think about coming to that meeting with me, next week? I won't pressurise you.'

'I promise I'll think about it,' she said, just as Emily arrived back at the table. 'Now then, poppet,' she said, 'which pie would you like me to order for you?'

***

The rest of the time in the pie shop was focused purely on Emily and her needs and wants but every so often, Tobias caught Cassie's eye and she smiled at him until finally, he dipped his hand into his pocket and brought out some coins. 'I'll just settle the bill as there's somewhere I need to be,' he said cheerfully. Then rising from his seat, he came around to Cassie's side of the table and placed a hand on her shoulder and whispered in her ear. 'Think on about what I said, won't you?' Having him at such close proximity caused a tingle of excitement to run down her spine. This was so wrong though and she realised it. He pulled away unexpectedly and ruffling Emily's hair said, 'See you, poppet! Now you be a good girl for your mother, won't you?'

Emily nodded and smiled and then waved at him as he left to pay at the counter. A sudden feeling of loss hit Cassie in the pit of her stomach. What if she were to take the children and go to America with Tobias? Would Harry miss her that much? None of the children was his anyhow. He was a good father to them as in being a good provider but he never really got all that involved with any of them, though she couldn't doubt that he did have a kind of love for them. But to be fair to him, Marshfield Coal Pit and his book store took up a lot of his time as well as being concerned about his mother's welfare.

She must have stared at the pie shop door for such a long time after Tobias departed as Emily was tugging on her sleeve. 'Mama! Why aren't you listening to me?'

Bringing herself back into the present moment, she said, 'Sorry, Emily. I was far away there. What were you saying to me?'

'Were you thinking about that man, Tobias?' Emily looked up at her with wide eyes.

What could she say to that? 'I suppose I was, poppet.'

'What were you thinking about him?' Emily rested her head on her hands at the table and studied her mother's face.

'I was thinking what a lovely man he is.'

'That's good,' said Emily 'as I think he's a nice man too.'

'Oh, darling...' Cassie buried her head in her daughter's hair and hugged her close, realising that Emily never even said such a thing about Harry. To her, he was some dim and distant stranger who occasionally appeared at mealtimes, and in truth, that's how Harry was beginning to feel to Cassie too: a dim and distant stranger.

**

The wedding date was set for Saturday the 30th of September at St. Michael's Church. Polly and Aunt Bertha had made the wedding dress between them, Aunt Bertha couldn't do so much as a seamstress these days though her eyesight was significantly better than it had been before Cassie had taken her to get her sight checked and new glasses from the oculist at Hocklea. But still, she'd been able to instruct Polly on what to do and help with the fitting of the dress. The bridal gown was one of Cassandra's gowns that she'd brought with her from Marshfield Manor. It had been cut to fit

Rose's figure and pretty Belgian lace added to both that and one of Rose's old bonnets. She did look a picture and all though it had puzzled Cassandra why after the initial fitting it was then taken out a little at the seams, but maybe since working at the tea room the girl had gained some weight, she surmised as, after all, they often got to eat some of the left-overs or cakes that had become a little stale from time to time.

But something was bothering Rose, Cassie could tell. Her work at the tea room was suffering too as often she'd catch the girl staring out of the window or twisting her handkerchief between her fingers. Then there were the "huddled in the corner moments" between Rose and Doris as she caught them whispering with one another as though there was a special secret that the rest of the world wasn't privy to. She'd ask Rose casually on occasion how she was and she'd always reply that she was absolutely fine and things were going well for both her and Clyde.

Men! Why do they have to be the bane of our lives? Maybe Rose is still pining for Tobias? I can see what she sees in him. He's so unlike the other men around here. He's handsome, intelligent, rebellious and has a wicked charm about him. Cassie! What are you thinking?

Since bumping into Tobias and him accompanying her and Emily to the pie shop, she thought of nothing else except what he'd had to say about his thoughts on emigrating to America.

Imagine though if she upped sticks and left to go with him, taking all three children with her. Would Harry even notice she'd gone? Of course, he would, he'd probably be devastated, but still, at the back of her mind was the thought she could escape this mundane life for an exhilarating one in America. There she'd be free to pursue a teaching career as Tobias would support that dream in a way Harry wasn't doing here in Wakeford. Whatever else happened, she wanted to attend that emigration meeting at Hocklea Town Hall next week, even if just to see what it was all about.

Chapter Sixteen

Rose's father had indicated that the men were talking about her at The Ploughman's Arms and she'd suspected she was the subject of gossip herself when people came into the tea room, some customers had been looking at her strangely and muttering behind their open palms as they gazed in her direction. She'd tried to convince herself it was her imagination playing tricks but when her Pa had said he was glad that Clyde would make an honest woman out of her as she was soiled goods, she'd been devastated. But who would have put the word out? Had Tobias been boastful about his conquest? After all, it was nothing to him as he was a man of the world and well-experienced in such matters and it could easily slip out if he became inebriated. Doris? No, Doris had sworn faithfully she'd not tell a soul. She didn't doubt the girl. Suddenly, her hand flew to her mouth. *Mrs Hewitt!* She'd confided in her? No one else knew about her shenanigans, not even Polly. It had to be Cassandra Hewitt. But why tell folk and then give her a beautiful gown like that as a wedding gift? It made no sense. Still, she had a right to know, so the next morning when they were working together at the tea room, she asked to see the woman in confidence.

Cassie, as if realising something was up, asked Polly to take charge. They could cope for a few minutes as Doris was due in sometime soon. She led the girl out to the backyard. 'What's the matter?' she frowned as she gazed into her eyes. 'You've not been right in a long time and keep telling me all is fine with you? But I know there's something up!'

Rose trembled as she spoke to her employer. 'Mrs Hewitt, I have to ask you this, but did you tell anyone at all that I had relations with Tobias Beckett after I confided in you that time?'

Cassie shook her head. 'No, I've kept my word to you. What's the matter then?' She gazed deep into Rose's eyes.

'It's folk,' said Rose in desperation, 'they've been gossiping about me. I've noticed how the customers are looking at me sometimes and whispering and nudging one another, almost as though they're making fun of me.'

'Oh, surely not!' said Cassie shaking her head. 'It must be your imagination, Rose.'

'No, I'm telling you. It's getting worse, and my father has got wind of it at The Ploughman's Arms as well. Though no name has been mentioned as to who has had relations with me.'

'That is serious,' said Cassie. 'Maybe the sooner you are wed to Clyde the better. It might put a stop to all the gossip then.'

Rose bit her bottom lip as her eyes filled up with tears as she turned away for a moment. 'The trouble is, I haven't told you the full truth, nor Clyde either. He knows nothing about my intimate relations with Tobias and he knows nothing about this baby, either!' She patted her stomach as she turned back towards Cassie. And for the first time Rose realised, she couldn't hide her small bump much longer. Thankfully, Clyde hadn't noticed up until now as she was careful what she wore to disguise it.

Cassie's eyes enlarged. '*You mean you are pregnant after all*?'

Rose nodded slowly. 'I'm sorry I lied to you,' she sobbed.

'But it's not me who you need to be sorry to, Rose, it's Clyde. You have to tell him the truth! It would be unfair for him to marry you under these circumstances.'

'I can't. He'll disown me and then my baby won't have a father.' Rose protested.

'Then you must tell Tobias you are expecting his child, maybe he'll marry you then!' Rose looked at Cassie's face and she sensed this was upsetting her too for some reason.

'I'll have to think a bit longer,' Rose sniffed.

'Don't think too long, it's Monday today and you're getting wed on Saturday. You can't start married life on a lie, whatever were you thinking of?'

Rose realised that Cassie was very fond of Clyde

and wouldn't want to see him upset. 'I shall come to some sort of decision by then,' said Rose, shaking her head. 'I just have to as things can't go on like this.'

Cassie put her hand affectionately on the girl's shoulder and held her close while she wept her heart out. Maybe it was a daft idea of Doris's to con Clyde into believing he was the father of this child in the first place, though she realised she wouldn't have been the first young woman to do something like that. How many other men were there who believed a child was their own offspring when he or she wasn't?

* * *

Harry had arrived home early from pit business for a change and after the children were put to bed, he slipped his arms around Cassandra's waist from behind and snuggled into her back. It was a long time since he'd done anything like that.

She closed her eyes and inhaled his manliness and turned around to face him. The look in his eyes showed concern for her as he softly caressed her cheek as she gazed into his eyes, and at that moment, saw the great love he had for her there. How could she be so foolish even thinking of leaving him to travel halfway around the world? A shudder coursed her body as she was reminded of Mrs Beckett's prophecy. She'd seen a ship and travel. Maybe she'd even recognised the dark-haired man as being her son and that's why she'd stopped the session going any further. At least the potion the woman had supplied her with was now aiding a night of restful sleep.

'What is it, Cassandra?' Harry lifted her chin with his forefinger and thumb to gaze more deeply into her eyes.

Oh, she had to tell him, she simply had to. Taking a breath of composure and letting it out again, she said, 'I've felt the distance between us lately, Harry. Especially since you put me off my idea of training to become a teacher.'

Harry's mouth fell open. 'I had no idea,' he said with tears in his eyes. 'I didn't realise just how much it meant to you. If that's what it takes to make you happy then of course you must pursue your dream, my darling. I was trying to be practical, that was all.'

Cassandra began to weep in her husband's arms and when she'd finished, he carried her up the stairs to bed. She'd badly wanted to tell him what was going on with Clyde and Rose, he was his half-brother after all, but knowing Harry it would upset him to realise Clyde was about to be duped into a marriage that was based on a lie, and no doubt he'd then lay the blame at Tobias's door and that might be bad for all concerned.

**

It was now Thursday and Rose still hadn't decided whether to tell Clyde the truth or not or even whether she should inform Tobias he was about to become a father either. She confided in Doris, who seemed a little evasive with her.

'What on earth's the matter?' she asked the girl.

'I…I don't know how to tell you this,' Doris said, her eyes darting all over the place as if she were perplexed about something, 'that day you called to my house and we sat in the scullery discussing your news…'

'Yes, go on,' said Rose impatiently.

'My sister, Ruth, overheard us talking. She told me about it and I made her swear not to say a thing but it was too late by then, she'd already told her boyfriend, Billy, who went and got himself drunk at The Ploughman's Arms that night and he ended up spilling the beans to someone else who told a group of men there.'

Rose's mouth popped open in horror. 'Oh, my goodness!' she shrieked. 'I was right then, I wasn't imagining things. People have been speaking about me, I'm just going to have to leave this place right now.' Rose's eyes filled with tears as Doris draped a comforting arm around her.

'Perhaps you ought to tell Clyde the truth then and see what he says?' She proffered.

Rose shrugged her shoulders. Yes, it was the right thing to do, she realised that in her heart, but once she'd told him that might be it. It could be the end of their relationship forever and no father for her baby—no one to take care of them either.

'Mrs Hewitt said she thinks I should inform Tobias that he is about to become a father.'

Doris bit her bottom lip. 'I don't think that's a good idea at all!' she said stoically. 'He's already done a runner by having no more to do with you after you did the deed together. You don't need that kind of man in your life!'

Maybe what Doris said was true, but she did have to find out. 'I've got to know what he thinks though. Then if he rejects me a second time, maybe that's when I ought to tell Clyde the truth.'

'Sounds the best of a bad job,' Doris said, patting her friend on the back.

The trouble was when should she tell Tobias? And where? She couldn't exactly call at his home, she'd been there once before when everyone was out, so she knew where he lived but she had no plans to upset his family, particularly his mother who she realised he was close to. The news about the pregnancy might well devastate the woman, and in all honesty, if Tobias rejected her a second time, she'd have upset his mother for no reason at all as she'd never get to see her grandchild anyhow.

***

Rose and Doris had volunteered to stay on after work to give the tea room a good clean, they rolled up their sleeves to scrub the shelves and tables, mopped the floor and even washed the windows. If Cassie was surprised when they'd offered to do it, she hadn't said so but instead offered them anything they wished to take home from the tea room the next day as payment for their services.

Rose, though, had an ulterior motive. She knew that Tobias walked that way home from the pit and roughly the time too, so she and Doris kept watch for him passing. No way could she turn up at his home nor the coal pit. This had to be done in a decent manner on neutral ground. *Neutral ground?* She almost laughed at the thought of that, after all, it was here they had both done the deed in the first place that had led to all of this. Anyhow, she intended to inform him that she was pregnant and that she'd be marrying Clyde on the weekend.

If he thought anything of her, it would be his chance to say, *'No, don't you go marrying Clyde. I'm the man for you. You're carrying my child.'*

Was that what she really wanted? She'd thought long and hard about it. With Clyde she'd have a future and would want for nothing and he'd take care of her and the child, with Tobias, she wouldn't know what to expect but at least it would be exciting.

As darkness fell, Doris yelled, 'He's passing right now, Rose! Go and nab him and I'll make myself scarce in the backroom!'

Rose nodded and dashed out through the tea room door as she watched Tobias passing in the distance beneath the glow of the street lamp. He was in his work clothes and carrying his metal snap tin.

'Tobias!' she shouted.

He turned to face her and she closed the distance between them as breathlessly she approached him.

'Hello, Rose!' he said, knocking back the peak of his flat cap with his hand as if to get a better view of her in the semi-darkness. 'How are you keeping?'

'That's what I wanted to speak to you about, Tobias,' she said softly. 'There's something I need to say to you.'

'Oh, what's this?' he chuckled and then his voice took on a serious tone as he said, 'Hey, you're not after what happened last time again, are you? As I can't.'

Confused, she shook her head. 'No, it's words I have to say not things I have to do.'

He nodded. 'Very well,' he said and he followed her back to the tea room.

Once inside, she locked the door behind them, noticing that Tobias's actions were very guarded. This didn't seem to be the same man who only a couple of short months ago had been so passionate and hot for her. Now he appeared cold and distant but nevertheless, she just had to find out what he thought about her and the baby.

'It's like this you see, Tobias, have you ever thought any more about me and you?'

'Me and you?' He frowned. 'Rose, there is no me and you. There never was really.'

She felt a lump rising in her throat. 'B...but we stepped out together. Then finally we became one.'

'You were just too clingy for me, Rose!' he said, now raising his voice. 'I need my space!'

Rose held her chin high. 'And haven't I given that to you? You've had plenty of space when I've not bothered you at all despite...' as she said the words she realised something. Why had she never seen it before? 'There's someone else, isn't there?'

He removed his flat cap and lowered his head for a moment until slowly, he raised it to look in her eyes. 'Yes. Yes, there is.'

Rose felt as though her heart might burst. 'But I gave you everything! All of me!' she cried as she pummelled at his chest with both fists as he tried to keep her at bay by grabbing hold of her wrists. Then she was in his arms, sobbing as he caressed her and held her to him. Oh, it was still there, she loved him but he didn't love her.

Sniffing, she lifted her head to look up at him. 'And you love her?'

'Yes, I do, Rose. Very much indeed. We both won't be around here much longer, we're going away together,' he said.

At that moment, Rose hated the other woman whoever she was for taking him away from her. If she didn't exist then Tobias might be hers right now. 'Who is she?' she demanded through clenched teeth, with her hands balled into fists.

'I'm not at liberty to tell you that,' he said shaking his head.

He was obviously trying to protect the woman whoever she was. All she could think of doing now was hurting him. 'Never mind. At least I now know what sort of a man you are, Tobias Beckett! I've called you in here to tell you something and by damn I'm going to say it!'

He stared at her in astonishment. It was obvious

he'd never seen her lose control before and she realised that her anger could frighten people at times when she finally let loose as mostly it was repressed. 'Let me tell you, I no longer need you in my life as on Saturday Clyde and I are getting wed at St. Michael's Church!'

'That's nice for you, both. Let me be the first to congratulate you!' He held out his hand to shake hers but she knocked it away.

'What most folk don't realise is that I'm pregnant!'

'Oh!' That had taken the wind out of his sails. 'W...well it's not the end of the world and you and Clyde can always tell people the baby is premature when he or she is born.'

Rose threw back her head and laughed. 'Oh, you think so? The thing is the baby isn't Clyde's! *It's yours!*'

She watched Tobias's jaw slacken. 'No, that can't be true, Rose. You'd have told me before now.'

'It's true. Every word of it. You can ask Mrs Hewitt, if you like.'

'Mrs Hewitt? What has she to do with it?'

'Because she's known from the beginning what happened between me and you. I lied to her at first and told her I'd made a mistake about being pregnant but finally, she knows the truth. It was her idea that I tell you before the wedding takes place at the weekend. Of course, I have to tell Clyde now and hope that he will still want to marry me.'

'Rose,' said Tobias as though he were thinking

things over. 'I don't know what to say. I'm sorry I've left you pregnant but I am prepared to take responsibility for the child.'

For a moment her heart swelled as she assumed he was going to say he'd marry her after all as the child now made a difference. 'You will?' she blinked several times.

'Yes, I can give you some money towards the child's upkeep, it's the least I can do.'

She stuck her chin out in defiance and placing her hands on her hips said, 'So, you'd pay towards the child but not take me on because you won't give this woman up?'

He nodded. 'Yes, precisely.'

'Then get out of here! The child and its mother want no more to do with you ever again!' She pointed towards the door as he began to protest.

'Please, Rose. We can work something out.'

'I've said all I am going to say about this, now go! Or otherwise, I'll march over to The Ploughman's Arms and get my father and brothers to throw you out!'

As if realising there was no more he could say or do, Tobias replaced his cap on his head and left the shop with his head bowed low and his shoulders hunched up like a beaten man. And didn't that feel good for Rose?

Hearing the door closing, Doris rushed out from the backroom. 'I can't believe what I just heard there!' she said folding her arms. 'Are you all right, Rose?'

'I think I am now,' said Rose huffing out a puff of exasperation.

'Yer dealt superbly with that situation. He had it coming to him that one!'

Rose nodded. 'Only thing is, I wonder who that other woman is and why he's so keen to protect her like that?'

'I dunno,' said Doris frowning. 'He obviously thinks the world of her whoever she damn well is!'

'Maybe we'll never find out if they're both going away together,' she sighed. 'One thing I do know now though is how foolish I was to get involved with Tobias Beckett in the first place. Clyde would have never treated me that way.'

'Got to agree with you there, gal. Don't let Clyde getaway, you'll never find another who loves you like he does.'

Rose nodded and then her eyes welled up with tears as her shoulders shook as she cried. 'Oh, what have I done, Doris? Clyde doesn't deserve any of this. I have got to tell him the truth.'

trouser pockets. 'I've told you before, I ain't the marrying kind. I'm a free spirit.'

'So, if I had decided to go to America with you, we'd have had to live tally?'

'Yes, initially, until you'd divorced your husband.'

Cassie couldn't believe the way he was speaking to her. 'Tobias, you have certainly gone down in my estimation.'

'Why?' He angled his head to one side as if puzzled.

'Because you're doing the dirty on Rose, that's why! Do I have to spell it out for you?'

'It's because of you though, Cassie.' He drew in a deep breath and let it out again. 'It's you I love! You're the only woman I'll ever love and Rose doesn't even come a close second to you. She's not fit to tie your shoelaces.'

Tobias stepped forward and took her in his arms as she did her best to resist but then his lips were on hers as he plundered her mouth and she gave up resisting as he traced the contours of her breast with his free hand.

This couldn't be happening to her. She seemed powerless to resist for a while but then she came to her senses. No! This isn't what she wanted.

'Get off!' she shouted as she pushed him away. 'I love Harry! Now please leave me alone!'

As if surprised by his actions, he pulled away and raising his vertical palms said, 'I am so sorry I did that, I misjudged the situation. You and Mr

Hewitt have been so good to me an' all.' For a moment, she thought she saw his eyes fill with tears, but he turned away and clambered back over the wall, making his way onto the path in front of the cottage that would take him back to Wakeford.

Cassie heaved out a sigh of relief. Thank goodness she had come to her senses when she had. At least no harm was done. It had just been a kiss that had decided things for her once and for all. It was over for them both.

**

Rose had left the tea room to pay Cassie a visit to inform her that she had finally told Tobias about the baby. It was as if a load had been removed from her shoulders. Maybe Mrs Hewitt would invite her inside for a quick chat before returning to work.

As she walked along the path towards the cottage, she noticed someone leaving in a hurry, taking large strides towards her.

Tobias!

Before he had a chance to see her, she hid behind a tree. What had he been doing at Rose Cottage? Mr Hewitt wouldn't be there right now as Rose realised the man was at work.

Cassie! Why hadn't she seen it before? She was the other woman. The woman who Tobias was keen to protect. How could they both carry on in such a fashion? Harry Hewitt was one of the most handsome men in the whole of Wakeford and a hardworking man too. What a Jezebel! And her having three young children and all.

She gave Tobias time to pass before tailing him back to Wakeford where she watched him enter The Ploughman's Arms. Shocking at this time of day and all! Her brothers she'd expect it of but not him. She'd ask them later if he'd said anything to them or what sort of mood he'd been in.

For time being, she was going to return to the tea room to tell Doris what she'd just seen to see what she'd make of it all, realising she couldn't face Mrs Hewitt right now after what she'd just discovered.

***

When Rose returned to the tea room, she ushered Doris outside to the yard while Polly was preoccupied sorting out the tea urn. There were no customers inside, so both girls knew they wouldn't be missed for a couple of minutes.

'You were quick!' said Doris.

'And no bloomin' wonder and all. When I got near Mrs Hewitt's place, guess who was just leaving with a face like thunder?'

Doris shrugged her shoulders. 'I dunno. Who?'

'Only Tobias!'

Doris appeared as if about to squeal with surprise, but she clamped her hand over her mouth to keep it under wraps. Then after a moment of quelling the shocked surprise, her eyes enlarged as she said, 'So, you think Tobias and Mrs Hewitt have been at it, like?'

'Sssh, keep your voice down in case Polly hears. Yes, it must be her, she's the other woman. I've been thinking about it and it all makes sense now why Tobias has been trying to protect her identity.'

'But if he said he was going away with this other woman, surely she wouldn't leave her three children behind? Two of them are only babies!'

Rose shook her head. 'I don't think she'd leave them, she'd take them with her. Don't forget, not one of those children is fathered by Mr Hewitt. Lord Bellingham, her previous husband, fathered those two kiddies. Don't know about Emily's father but I think Polly mentioned once that he'd passed away.'

'So, no real ties for our Mrs Hewitt then! She's a dark horse an' all!' Scoffed Doris.

'Isn't she just!' Rose's eyes were glinting now. 'I reckon if he hadn't fallen for her, he'd have married me! And to think all that time I've been confiding in her, the cow!'

Doris shot her a sharp sideways glance. 'Aw, you can't call Mrs Hewitt that, Rose. She's been good to us.'

'Good my backside!' Rose threw her arms up in the air. 'I've got a good mind to go and see Mr Hewitt to tell him what's been going on...'

As Rose's voice trailed away, neither girl had noticed Polly emerging through the backroom door. 'Tell Mr Hewitt about what?'

Rose's cheeks blazed. Feeling tongue-tied now, she wasn't sure what to say.

'It's about the meeting at The Ploughman's Arms, Miss Hedge. There's one on next week about some sort of strike action at the pit.' Doris folded her arms in a business-like fashion.

Polly frowned and shook her head as she tutted. 'Not again! For goodness sake! I bet I know who's behind it an' all—Tobias Beckett, the rabble-rouser!' Then she turned on her heel and left them to it, as the girls whispered about their suspicions regarding Mrs Hewitt and Tobias.

They were startled as a few minutes later, Polly shouted, 'Quick as you like, girls! I've got the tea urn going now and a couple of customers have just arrived.'

Rose looked thankfully at Doris. It was a pure lie of course but it had got her out of a sticky situation. The question was for now, what was she going to do with the information she had? Should she risk telling Mrs Hewitt's husband what had been going on when he was at work or should she keep quiet about it as she hadn't as yet made up her mind to tell Clyde about the baby before their upcoming wedding on the weekend?

Oh, what a dilemma!

***

Tobias had drunk far more at The Ploughman's Arms than he'd intended to. His original intention was to have a couple of pints of ale just to calm himself down after what had just occurred with Cassie, but everyone was buying him drinks and patting him on the back for all he'd done for the children at the pit and the mills. It was hard to refuse as he didn't want to upset anyone.

'Have another, Tobias!' Someone was shaking his hand.

'Good man!' An elderly man was patting his shoulder.

Tobias became aware of a man staring at him from across the bar. The man's gaze was fixed and inflexible. Then the man spoke in a loud manner. 'Well, look who we have here, Edmund!' That didn't sound like a friendly voice. Tobias's vision was becoming blurred as he struggled to bring his eyes into focus. The room was beginning to spin as he slurred his speech. Now he recognised the man: it was Daniel Barton stood beside Edmund, Rose's elder brothers. He realised what trouble he was in as both men began pushing their way through the crowd of men towards him.

Feeling himself being grabbed by the lapels of his jacket and lifted off his feet, the face leered ever closer to his. He could smell the man's beery breath. 'Now you've done a wrong thing by our Rose and you're going to do the right thing from now on, understood?'

'Yes,' echoed Edmund. 'You've despoiled our sister and if you don't want your features splattered all over the pavement outside, you'll do the right thing by her!'

Tobias gulped as some of the other men who had been congratulating him tried to intervene, but it was too late. He was dragged out of the pub, down the road, and into an alleyway by the brothers where he was pummelled with their fists.

Maybe he deserved this, but no, Rose had been as keen as he was, in fact, she had lured him to the tea room that night, so it just wasn't fair.

'Take advantage of a young woman, would you?' Daniel threw a fist in his face as Tobias reeled backwards in pain as he felt warm blood trickling down his nose.

'B...but I didn't force her to do anything,' protested Tobias as he did his best to remain on his feet as he swayed back and forth from the punch.

A gang of men had now emerged from the pub and were watching what was taking place. He heard one who had earlier congratulated him saying, 'And to think I bought that rotter a pint of ale earlier! He deserves all he gets if he forced himself on a young woman like that!'

'It's tantamount to rape!' shouted another.

***

As all this was going on, Rose had caught sight of Tobias being dragged away from the pub by her brothers from the tea room opposite. She'd fled leaving Polly and Doris wondering what on earth was going on.

Breathlessly, she pushed her way through the crowd of men, shouting, 'Leave him alone, you pair! You ought to be ashamed of yourselves! Two on to one like that!'

'It's a fair fight when the man's a bloody rapist!' Someone yelled at her.

Rose stared at Tobias's bloodied face, he could hardly stand up. Then turning to her brothers she said, 'Is that what you think? That he forced himself upon me?'

Daniel and Edmund released Tobias, whose body slid down the wall and onto the ground. They both nodded at her.

'Aye, yes,' said Daniel.

'No, it wasn't like that at all!' Cried Rose with tears in her eyes as she was forced to tell them what happened at a cost to herself. 'I loved him and I thought he loved me, so I gave myself to him. I thought he'd marry me after that!' Her face crumpled as she said the words which were like a dagger piercing her heart over and over again. Saying those words made it more real somehow and in front of everyone too. She'd never live it down but she didn't want Tobias marked as a rapist because whatever he was, he wasn't one of those.

Her brothers shook their heads as some of the men around muttered derogatory comments under their breath, but Rose was past caring what anyone thought of her now. 'Whatever he's done to me, he doesn't deserve this!'

Some of the men began to look a little embarrassed to be caught up in this and departed to go back inside The Ploughman's Arms. Finally, she was left with her brothers and Tobias who was slumped against the wall where they'd left him.

'But he should have done the decent thing and married you!' Accused Edmund.

Rose nodded. 'Aye, he should have but he's in

love with someone else.'

Her brothers both glared at her until Daniel finally asked, 'Who is he in love with?'

She watched Tobias's eyes and could see how sad they looked, he was imploring her not to say anything to them if she had any suspicions at all who the woman was.

'I don't know,' said Rose shaking her head. 'I don't much care either as I love Clyde, he's the man for me, I realise that now. I'll be marrying him on Saturday! My love for Tobias was crazy, something out of my control that swept me off my feet, but with Clyde I know he'll always love me and be there for me.' As she said the words, her heart went out to Tobias, she couldn't just switch off her feelings like that.

'Let's hope Clyde will want to marry you now after half the pub knows about your shenanigans with this one!' Daniel spat in Tobias's direction.

Realising she now had to put Clyde straight, Rose said, 'Well, if I lose him I lose him over this but I couldn't allow you to keep on beating Tobias. Whatever he's done to me, he doesn't deserve this! You might have beaten him to death.'

Briefly, both brothers looked ashamed of themselves but they didn't apologise for it, instead, they exchanged glances with one another and made off back in the direction of the pub so that Rose was left alone with Tobias. 'Come on,' she said offering her hand to enable him to get back onto his feet. 'I'll take you back to the tea room with me to get you cleaned up.'

Tobias looked up at her with tears in his eyes and smiled. 'You're too good to me,' he said as he accepted her hand and pulled himself onto his feet and then walked unsteadily in the direction of the tea room.

Chapter Eighteen

Doris stared at Rose in disbelief. 'You can't go bringing Tobias in here in that state!' She said through pursed lips.

'It's quiet enough at the moment,' Rose glanced around the tea room. There was only an elderly gentleman seated with his wife at a window table. 'Those are all the customers we have here at the moment and they're not taking the slightest bit of notice.'

Doris glanced at the pair who seemed deep in conversation with one another. 'Quick then,' she said hurriedly. 'Take him in the backroom before Polly returns.'

Rose quirked a curious brow. 'Where's she gone then, she was here before I left?'

'To be truthful,' Doris said in a conspiratorial tone, 'she reckoned she was popping out to the bakery for more bread, but I think she was trailing you to see where you were off to as you left here in a rush.'

'Oh!' Rose startled, she hadn't wanted to cause any bother when she'd dashed off like that. She took Tobias by the arm as she softly said, 'This way. We'll soon get you cleaned up.' Then turning to Doris she said, 'Bring me a bowl of warm water, Doris. Use the tea urn as that's been boiled. Oh, and a clean cloth.'

Doris did what was asked of her and soon, Tobias was seated in the backroom having his wounds carefully attended to by Rose.

'So, what happened at Cassie's cottage earlier?'

Tobias winced as she patted the damp cloth near his eye which was now sporting a large red bump that no doubt would end up purple soon. He looked up at her as she stepped away from him. 'You know about that?'

'Er, not exactly. I went to see Mrs Hewitt and got the shock of my life to see you leaving the cottage. You looked sort of upset so I hid and followed you back to the pub. That's how I discovered my brothers were battering you.'

He shot her a half-smile before tenderly touching his jaw. 'Aye, they nearly knocked the life out of me there. They both pack a mean punch.' Then his smile disappeared. 'I went to see Cassie as I'd told her about how an Emigration Agent had arranged a meeting in the town hall at Hocklea next week to sign up folk who want to go to America to work.'

Rose gasped. For a moment, she didn't know whether she believed him or not. 'But why would you go there when you have a perfectly good job at the coal pit?'

'Because,' he lifted his head to look up at her, 'there are good opportunities there for someone

he lusted after me.'

Harry nodded. 'But what about Tobias, you said you had drawn close to him? Has anything happened between you? I have to admit I couldn't bear it if you were in love with him.'

She smiled and shook her head. 'No, I'm not in love with him, I realise that now. I was infatuated with him as he was so passionate about things. *But he's in love with me.*'

'Oh!' Harry's eyebrows rose in surprise. 'But he's quite a bit younger than you.'

'I am aware of it. He had mentioned that he might emigrate to America, did you know that?'

'No, I didn't. So, he would be out of the picture anyhow and leaving you behind, so what's the problem?'

She shook her head and began to sob as she said through shuddering breaths, 'He wanted to take me with him.'

'No!' shouted Harry. 'Never! I would fight to the death for you, Cassandra. I love you so much.'

'I realise that, Harry. Don't worry, I am not going to leave you, but he called around here later for my answer and he kissed me. Then I told him no, I wasn't going with him as I love you!'

'Oh, Cassandra...' He shook his head and tears filled his eyes.

'Can you forgive me?' She paused to look into her husband's eyes before continuing. 'I realised as he kissed me it wasn't what I wanted, what I wanted was you.'

Harry smiled as a tear trickled down his cheek. 'Of course I can forgive you. I feared for a moment that you were going to say you wanted to leave me. I could never bear that.'

'Nor could I,' she sniffed.

'But promise me one thing?'

'Anything? Name it?'

'That you must never keep any secrets from me ever again. I don't mean the sort of nice secrets, like a gift for my birthday or something like that. I mean deep, dark secrets. You should have told me immediately about what happened with Anthony Fairley. I've a good mind to horsewhip the brute!'

'No, please don't, Harry,' she implored. 'As it is, I know I can hold it over him if we need to get him on our side regarding any school issues. I'm sure he'll never try anything ever again.'

'He'd better not!' said Harry. 'But be sure that I'll inform James of this as he's my business partner and he needs to know the sort of man we're dealing with here.'

'Very well.' She huffed out a long breath, feeling like the weight of the world had been removed from her shoulders.

***

When Tobias had left the tea room, Doris drew Rose to one side. 'I heard what he said to you in there. I hope you're not going to do anything foolish, are yer?'

Rose drew in a deep composing breath and let it out again. 'I don't know what to do, to be honest with you, Doris. I'm feeling a bit overwhelmed by it all.'

'Just you remember this, if you don't remember anything else at all. You're second choice, my girl! If Cassie had said "yes" to him he wouldn't have asked you at all.'

Rose's face crumpled almost as though she might cry for a moment but then she straightened her shoulders and as her chin jutted out in defiance, she said, 'That's as maybe but what has made a difference is Tobias knowing I'm carrying his child and the fact I just showed how much I cared for him when I might have left him to the mercy of my brothers.'

'What's that about your brothers?' Polly had returned to the tea room with a wicker basket containing loaves of bread hooked over the crook of her arm.

The girls were so immersed in their conversation they'd not heard her arrive as the door was propped open with a metal pail of water as Doris had been mopping up the floor while it was quiet, so the overhead bell hadn't jangled.

Rose's face blazed. 'I just rescued Tobias from my brothers who were in the midst of hammering the life out of him.' She admitted.

Polly exchanged glances with Doris almost as though she couldn't believe what Rose was saying.

'It's true,' confirmed Doris. 'It was over how he'd left Rose high and dry and now there's a baby on the way...'

Rose glared at her friend and as if realising she had slipped up, Doris clamped her hands over her mouth, before dropping them to her sides and saying, 'I'm sorry, Rose.'

'Don't worry,' said Rose. 'Everyone in The Ploughman's Arms will know about it now anyhow thanks to my brothers.'

'A baby?' said Polly. 'I never knew you were pregnant? I mean I realised there was something wrong some time ago when I suggested Cassie speak with you but I thought all was resolved and now you were getting on so well with Clyde. After all, your wedding is this weekend!'

'I was getting on famously with Clyde, Miss Hedge, but I'm sorry to admit this, but I was going to marry him and pretend Tobias's child was his.'

Polly's eyes enlarged as she shook her head and pursed her lips. 'I can't believe I'm hearing this. I thought better of you, Rose Barton! You have to tell Clyde the child's not his and hope he might forgive you, though I have to say, many men wouldn't given the circumstances.'

'That's not all though,' admitted Rose. 'Tobias now wants to marry me and has asked me to go to America with him!'

'Oh, me giddy aunt! I'm going to have to sit down a minute, I can't take all this in.' Polly placed the basket of bread on the counter and she drew out a chair and took a seat at one of the tables. Finally, after a moment's contemplation, she looked up at Doris and said, 'Go and make us all a pot of coffee while it's quiet, we need to discuss this and what Rose should do as she could be making a huge mistake whatever she decides to do.'

Doris nodded and she went about the task of brewing up the coffee while Rose joined Polly at the table.

***

Cassie's sleep was disturbed. Polly had called earlier to tell her the news about Rose, so she was forced to tell the woman her own involvement with Tobias and how in the end she'd set him straight after that kiss in the garden.

Cassie was dreaming that it was the day of Rose and Clyde's wedding. Dark, ominous clouds had gathered over the spire of St. Michaels and there was a sense of foreboding before the service had even begun. The interior of the church was packed out with wedding guests all happy to see the wedding taking place. But as the couple was exchanging their vows and the vicar was asking if anyone had any objection as to why the wedding should take place, a lone figure arrived at the open front door of the church. There were gasps from the congregation as Tobias Beckett, who cut a dashing figure in a silver-grey long coat, white shirt, with silver-grey cravat and matching top hat strode purposely down the aisle towards the pulpit. Cassie gasped as he hesitated at the end of her pew as she clung on to Harry's hand, closed her eyes and buried her head in her husband's chest.

But then she heard footsteps as Tobias carried on walking up to the pulpit. The vicar had stopped mid-sentence and there was a deathly hush as he peered over his glasses from the wooden lectern. Rose, who in the dream was wearing a white satin dress, not the one she'd had gifted her, turned to face Tobias as Clyde stood there looking uncertain.

'You're coming with me,' said Tobias firmly as he held out his hand towards Rose. 'You belong to me —both you and our child!'

Cassie had risen to her feet and shouted from the pew. 'No! Leave her alone! Go to America on your own, Tobias!'

The congregation had gasped and turned towards Cassie and stared hard at her. A woman in the pew in front, who she didn't recognise, turned towards her and asked, 'How do you know he's off to America then?'

Cassie had looked at the woman and replied, 'He told me so himself because he asked me to go with him first!'

Then, one-by-one, the people stood to stare at Tobias as they pointed at him and chanted, 'Rabble-rouser!' 'Rabble-rouser!' 'Rabble-rouser!'

All hell broke loose as they tossed thorny red roses at Rose as drops of blood splattered her white wedding gown.

'No!' Cassie was shouting. 'That could have been me!'

It was then Harry woke her, gently rousing her from what she was relieved to discover had been a nightmare for her. Then he'd taken her into his arms and rocked her back to sleep.

Chapter Nineteen

Tobias did not show his face at Marshfield Coal Pit ever again. The men were confused and a little puzzled as he was such a committed worker there and the best foreman they'd ever had. A meeting was summoned outside the pit entrance by the men headed by Abraham Mason to ask if anyone knew of his whereabouts, but none did, except for one young man who stepped forward.

'What is it, Bobby? Are you aware of something?' Abraham asked as the other men looked on.

The lad lowered his head and when he raised it again, his eyes looked guarded. 'Rumour I heard that's all. Gossip. Doubt there's any truth in it though.' He absently kicked a piece of coal that had fallen off a large pile beside him.

'Go on, lad, spit it out!' Urged Billy Crowther. He was one of the older men who told it like it was and had no time for messing about.

'It were me elder brother, see...' Bobby began. 'Our Stanley. He was at The Ploughman's Arms the other afternoon when a disturbance broke out involving Tobias.'

'Oh, aye?' said Abraham, cocking his head to one

side as if pondering things.

'He was dragged away by Rose Barton's elder brothers and apparently, they set on him in the alleyway. By all accounts, they were giving him a good pasting but Rose stepped in and stopped them.'

'That doesn't explain why he's not at work though!' said Billy sharply.

'Give the lad a chance to finish what he's telling us!' Abraham glared in Billy's direction.

'Well, the talk was at the pub later, and Tobias did not return, nor the brothers, that Tobias had got Rose in the family way and was refusing to marry her. That's why her brothers laid into him.'

'It all makes sense now,' said Abraham rubbing his stubbled chin. 'I'll have to have a word with the bosses later as if Tobias has thrown in a good job and left here without saying, he'll need replacing.'

'You could do that job, Abraham!' Someone in the crowd shouted.

There were murmurs of agreement but Abraham held up his vertical palm. 'Enough for now! I won't be taking anyone's job for time being, we need to get to the bottom of this first. But if Tobias has left here and doesn't want his job any longer, then I will happily step into his shoes, though they are large ones to fill.'

The men nodded and then they made their way into the pit carrying their lamps and metal snap tins. None of them could afford to lose too much time wondering and worrying about someone like

Tobias Beckett, no matter how well he'd done for them and their cause. There was work to be done.

After his shift, Abraham called to see the bosses at the office and was informed by James Wilkinson that a letter had arrived that morning from Tobias giving his notice to quit with immediate effect.

Abraham stood there with his cap in his hand. 'I still don't understand,' he said, scratching his head. 'I thought he liked it here and he did a lot for our Alfie which me and the missus are both grateful for.'

James nodded. 'I know,' he said sombrely. 'Mr Hewitt has informed me though that there's word that he's off to America. He's meeting with an emigration agent in Hocklea next week.'

'Oh, I see,' said Abraham. 'I had heard that colliers do well out there as they have skills to offer.'

'Apparently so.' James nodded.

'Is it all right if I tell the men then what you've told me?'

'Yes, that's absolutely fine, Abraham. The only trouble is now, he'll need replacing. Have you any idea who could do his job to his standard?'

Abraham paused for a moment before finding the words to say. 'I'm not saying I'd be as good as Tobias Beckett, Mr Wilkinson, but the men wanted me to put myself forward.'

'Splendid!' said James with a smile. 'I rather hoped you'd say that. I'll inform Mr Hewitt later. This will of course mean a pay rise for you which

Books by Lynette Rees

<u>Historical</u>

The Seasons of Change Series

Black Diamonds

White Roses

Blue Skies

Red Poppies

Winds of Change Series

The Workhouse Waif

The Matchgirl

A Daughter's Promise

The Cobbler's Wife

Rags to Riches Series

The Ragged Urchin

The Christmas Locket

The Lily and the Flame

The Wakeford Chronicles

The Widow of Wakeford

A Distant Dream

Act of Remembrance

Copyright

Printed in Great Britain
by Amazon